FOR THE LOVE OF BLOOD 2

Jamel Mitchell

Lock Down Publications and Ca$h Presents

For the Love of Blood 2

A Novel by *Jamel Mitchell*

For the Love of Blood 2

Lock Down Publications
Po Box 944
Stockbridge, Ga 30281

Visit our website @
www.lockdownpublications.com

Copyright 2022 by Jamel Mitchell
For the Love of Blood 2

Lock Down Publications
Like our page on Facebook: Lock Down Publications @
www.facebook.com/lockdownpublications.ldp
Book interior design by: **Shawn Walker**
Edited by: **Kiera Northington**

Stay Connected with Us!

Text **LOCKDOWN** to 22828 to stay up-to-date with new releases, sneak peaks, contests and more…
Thank you.

Submission Guideline.

Submit the first three chapters of your completed manuscript to ldpsubmissions@gmail.com, subject line: Your book's title. The manuscript must be in a .doc file and sent as an attachment. Document should be in Times New Roman, double spaced and in size 12 font. Also, provide your synopsis and full contact information. If sending multiple submissions, they must each be in a separate email.

Have a story but no way to send it electronically? You can still submit to LDP/Ca$h Presents. Send in the first three chapters, written or typed, of your completed manuscript to:

LDP: Submissions Dept
Po Box 944
Stockbridge, Ga 30281

DO NOT send original manuscript. Must be a duplicate.

Provide your synopsis and a cover letter containing your full contact information.

Thanks for considering LDP and Ca$h Presents.

DEDICATIONS

All Praise is due to Allah and Allah alone. To my wonderful family that has held me down
through the roughest times. I applaud you for your perseverance, your patience and unwavering
loyalty. I love you momma, Meela, Jamey, Jordy, Empress, King, Keem, Wink, Thugga, Lynitrah and Katie.
Words can't explain my gratitude. I can't thank you enough.

In Loving Memory of Terrell Delaquan Mac Davenport.
I promised you that I would finish this story no matter how long it took me to write it. You were always one of my greatest critics man, and I miss you dearly lil bruh. Taken too early from us all. I have you in prayer and faith. May peace be upon you. I love you my nigga..
This book is dedicated to your memory

ACKNOWLEDGEMENTS

If I forgot you in my first shout out I sincerely apologize. I can't forget the females that did have a nigga hand when times was at their roughest. You are not forgotten. Mikaela, the friendship we hold is amazing and I'm very grateful for you. I know you're missing Rell just as much as I am.

Saying thank you seems like an understatement for some of you. All I ask is that you keep spreading positivity, hope, love and loyalty. So for those I missed I wanna give a shout
of thanks. .. Destiny Morris, Jazmine L. , Keona, Jasmine L , Nadjula, Danielle, Virginia, Alyra,
Ivory (Marra), Beba, Amanda, Naeshia, and Tierra.

But I wanna give a special thank you to my beautiful lovelies Meechie.. Janasia.. Samiyah and
Mrz. Brittany... Thank you .. thank you .. thank you...

Now of course I can't forget my niggaz that goes through this every day struggle we call LIFE.

Shalor... Lil Malik... Snow... Chummy...Kev.. Lil Chris.. AD... Danna... Dez... Curt...

Rodo. . .Gaddy.. Millie, JDK, J Smoovie, Yayo, Radee, DC Show, and my nigga Black Tay.

Thank you my niggaz for remaining loyal to the cause !

Being locked up for as many calendars that I have been you see and meet people at a fast pace,

actually being able to call some ya friends is a challenge. The characters you meet in these places

are of the imagination. (Only if you knew) I'm very blessed to be able to call on ya'll.

I would also like to thank you Ca$h and my LOCK DOWN PUBLICATIONS family for your faith

in my craft. I promise to feed the streets fire after fire.

Courtlandt Ave. Stand Up !!!

Jamel Mitchell

Chapter One

Blatttt—tatt—tatt—tatt

The rapid gunfire dropped Simfany to the floor. She instinctively reached for her waist, but her gun was not on her person. *"Fuck! Fuck! Fuck!"* she cussed herself as she lay face down. When the gunfire ceased, she began crawling through the house. Simfany refused to die in a city that wasn't her own.

No bullets threatened the foundation of Carol's townhouse. The millisecond of calm allowed Simfany to gather the courage to make her move. She sprang to her feet, ran to her room and grabbed her gun a few seconds before another burst of gunshots erupted. She hit the floor once again, but now she had her gun in hand. Although she was shaken up, she was prepared to kill or be killed.

Silence followed this second burst of gunfire, then Simfany heard the unmistakable sound of tires squealing. She was confused about what had just taken place. She placed her back against the wall, anticipating more gunshots, but they never came. After a long moment of silence and still, she braved her way to the bedroom window. When she parted the curtains and looked out, all she saw was shards of glass and spent bullet casings in the ground. She cautiously continued to look up and down the main street. After determining that the shooter was gone, she breathed a sigh of relief.

She covered herself as she sparked a blunt and laid back. She was tired as fuck and desperately needed some sleep, but too much was going on for her to focus on closing her eyes and resting. Her mind raced. *None of this shit makes sense. How did Dracula know Carlos? How was Jim Dog involved with Byrd? I don't know what to make of what just happened!* she thought After an hour of futility, she gave up trying to answer those questions in her head. Only time could provide those answer, she decided. Exhausted, Simfany finally succumbed to sleep.

***

Detective Lawson nervously sped down Route 40, switching lanes back and forth, keeping his eyes on his rearview mirror. He needed to know that he wasn't being followed. He was happy to have escaped that encounter with his life. The image of the shooter holding the assault rifle on him flashed in his mind once again. He had thought he was going to be killed right there on the spot. His quick reaction had saved him. Instead of losing his life, the detective had only suffered a shattered windshield and a bullet-ridden car.

Once he felt safe, he pulled over and took a deep breath, thanking the heavens above for his escape. Then he picked up his folder and wrote a note to Ramos in case he got killed. Thinking about the ordeal as he began writing, Lawson realized that he was lucky that the would-be murderer had wanted to look him in the eyes before turning his lights out. Otherwise, he would've been a goner.

A moment later, after finishing the letter, Lawson made a mental note not to speak about the shooting and the connections until the timing was ideal. This was a career-changing case, and he was determined not to blow it. The shooting intensified his interest in the Parks and Vasquez pair. But had Lawson truly realized the danger he was getting into, he might've fell back and left it in God's hands. Because the only law in the streets was: *kill or be killed*.

***

Simfany woke up for the second time that day to the ringing of a phone; it was late in the day this time around. Simfany reached over and grabbed the phone from its cradle.

"Hello?" Simfany answered as she sat up and wiped the sleep out of her eyes. The voice on the other end of the phone was a pleasant one.

"May I speak to Ms. Vasquez? This is in regard to the two-bedroom townhouse located in the Edgewood area of the county. Is she in right now?" the woman on the other side of the phone asked.

"This is she," Simfany replied.

"Oh, okay. Well, hi. My name is Wanda Dawson. I'm a house representative here at Windsor Valley. We received all the paperwork this afternoon and you were happily accepted. If you're still interested, we have an opening for you. Please come to our office whenever you're available."

"Thank you. I will be there this afternoon to sign the papers and give you my deposit with the first six months' rent."

"Okay. I'll see you then. Drive safely." Simfany was excited to finally have her own space back. She loved Carol with all her heart, but a girl needed her own spot. She walked around the house as if she had a new lease on life. The *Juicy Couture* booty shorty she wore couldn't hold her ass in place as she danced throughout the apartment. With a big smile plastered across her face, she ran into Carol coming out of the kitchen.

"Bitch, what you so happy about?" Carol asked. Carol was caramel-skinned with doe-like eyes and the body of a goddess. Carol Washington was a unique sight to most.

"They finally called from Windsor Valley."

Carol laughed.

"Bitch, what's so funny?" Simfany asked, slightly irritated.

"Baby, no one calls it Windsor Valley with your corny ass. It's called Meadowood. Why would you move to the heart of the hood if you just moved out of West Baltimore? That makes no sense. A nigga just got killed out there a couple of nights ago."

"Shit! I'll be okay. Can't be any worse than New York. It's only until Santana comes home anyway. Thanks for putting me on point though. I now know what to expect." Simfany knew it wouldn't be a suburban kind of place, but it would have to do for now. Moving back to the heart of the hood wasn't what she wanted, though.

"It ain't that bad in Edgewood, Simfany. Shit! Meadowood ain't as violent as The Ville. That's where all the gangs are located mostly. You should be okay. You might even like it. It's better than living here in Hill Top. These Girard Street niggas get on my muthafucking nerves."

Carol patted her hair. Still feeling the itch, she began to scratch the spot.

"I hear that. I'm going back home when Santana gets out. I got to go out there to meet these people regarding this town house. I'll see you later, love." Simfany kissed Carol on her cheek and left the kitchen to get dressed for her meeting with Wanda Dawson.

As Simfany made her way into the main office in Windsor Valley, she was greeted by Ms. Dawson.

"And you are?" Ms. Dawson asked.

"Simfany Vasquez," she answered, noticing the look in Ms. Dawson's eyes. The look sent chills down her spine. Simfany saw past her fake smile and overbite. The look was the look of an insecure woman. *I got that type of effect on bitches.* Simfany smiled at her conceited thoughts.

"Oh, yeah. We got all the paperwork for you right here in my office. Please have a seat and I'll get to you as soon as I can. Thank you." Ms. Dawson motioned Simfany to one of the four chairs in the living room space. Simfany sat down and looked around. The office was exactly like the apartment she looked at only months earlier; the only difference was the color of the carpet. All the office was in reality a town house with a desk in the living room and offices upstairs. *Ghetto.* Simfany laughed. In no time Ms. Dawson came for her. Simfany grabbed her belongings and followed Ms. Dawson upstairs to her office. The office was spacious; Simfany admired that. She had to admit she was wrong about the office.

"Thank you for coming in, Ms. Vasquez. We have both homes you looked at. Do you prefer any one specifically? If so, please let me know." Ms. Dawson looked down at the paper work. She glanced back up when she received no answer.

"Ms. Vasquez?" Ms. Dawson called out, bringing Simfany out of her daze.

"Damn, my bad, ma'am. I was lost in thought. It doesn't really matter. I'd like to be tucked in the cut if possible. But whatever you pick is fine with me," Simfany said, as she went into her purse and pulled out the money order for the first six months' rent and deposit. Each month's rent was $750 and the deposit was $600. The money order made out to Windsor Valley was for $5,100. She handed the money order over to Ms. Dawson. She waited on the papers that she had to sign. The house rep hurried and filed the money before Simfany had the chance to change her mind. When Ms. Dawson was done, she began explaining the terms and rules of the complex.

"Again, thank you for choosing to reside here. You should like it. It's very close to all the establishments in Edgewood. It is also the calmest neighborhood in Harford County. Don't get me wrong. Things happen here, but nothing to fear. Anyway, these papers are the lease and the agreement to follow the rules that I just explained. No pets—etc.—things like that. While you go over the rules. I will make a copy of your money order. I'll be right back." Ms. Dawson left the room.

Bum ass bitch. Simfany sat and waited for Ms. Snobby to return. When Ms. Dawson came back, she returned with a copy of the lease, a copy of her payment and the keys to her new home.

"Thank you very much. I appreciate the welcoming." Simfany flashed a fake smile.

"The town house you will be occupying is 542 Meadowood Drive. It's located on the main drive. I'll show you where it is if you need me to."

"Nah, I'm good. Thank you. You've done enough." And just like that Simfany showed herself out. As Simfany made her way to the parking lot, she saw that the five hundred numbers were located across the street from the rental office. 542 was only a block away. Simfany laughed at her sudden humor. *Awwww! Ms. Dawson wants to keep an eye on me,* she teased.

"Fuck you, hoe!" she thought out loud.

Simfany readied herself for the drive back to Hill Top. Everything she owned that mattered was still in her West Baltimore home on Edmondson and Carey. She thought about leaving all her stuff behind and buying new things. Plus the money she got from Byrd and Emilio was hidden inside the residence. She would make the trip with movers, she told herself as she drove down route 40 back to Havre De' Grace. As soon as Simfany pulled out of the parking lot, Wanda picked the phone up and placed a call.

"Speak!" the voice on the other end of the phone demanded.

"542 Meadowood," was all that was needed to be said.

"Say no more. Good looking, shorty."

Simfany made the trip to Baltimore the next day. She made a quick decision to come without the movers. Her plan was to get all the things she needed and leave; the mover was   to come later in the day to retrieve the rest of her things. When Simfany pulled up to the town house in her 2002 Chevy Tahoe, a sudden sickness fell over her. The night she got shot flashed through her mind, body and soul. Simfany didn't want to be there, but it was a must. She sat in her truck and took three deep breaths. She reached into the glove compartment and pulled out the Glock 17 that rested there. She always kept a gun close before. Ever since that shooting incident that nearly took her life, she made a vow to always keep a gun on her person. Simfany was caught slipping not once but twice. After she was shot, she promised to die with her pistol. Simfany checked how much the magazine had; the clip indicated that it was sixteen shots ready to fly if need be. Simfany put the gun in the holster she had clipped to her waist. She pulled her Pelle Pelle leather jacket on and just sat in the driver seat looking down Carey Street. She took another deep breath and exited the car. It was an unusually quiet morning. The fiends were still out. Besides the drug trade, there was no traffic coming or going. It was fine with her; she only needed ten minutes of peace to grab her shit and go. Simfany sped-walked to the stairs of the town house and opened the door. She looked both ways before she entered the residence. Being paranoid became a natural feeling for Simfany, but she didn't let her uneasiness control her life. Being shot had a big effect on how she viewed her surroundings. Simfany knew it was do or die, so she stayed on her toes at all times.

As Simfany stepped into the house, she looked down at the carpet in the front door. The brown stain where she bled was still there. Simfany wasted no time; she locked the door and walked up the stairs. The money she acquired over the years was stashed in Santana's room. She smiled.

Only if that little nigga knew he was sleeping on more than a quarter of a million dollars, she thought. She walked over to a chair that was in the room, and took her jacket off. She even took the Glock off her hip, but she made sure it was still in reach. Simfany walked over to Santana's king-size bed and lifted it with all her strength. The bed sat up sideways as she held on to it. She pushed the mattress up against the wall to hold for support. The money was in the box spring.

That was also a trait she picked up from her beloved Dracula. When she turned around, she noticed a box of bullets and some money that sat on top of the box spring. She shook her head as she picked up the bullets and pocketed the money. *My baby boy grew up too fast*, she thought. But she knew she was the cause.

Simfany walked to the dresser and sat the bullets on top of it. Simfany looked back at the box spring; she needed something to cut into the wool top. She searched Santana's room for something sharp but came up empty. Simfany picked up her gun and walked to the kitchen in search of a knife. After she went down and retrieved the knife, she came back to the room and slit all four corners of the box spring. Simfany then carefully sliced an X from corner to corner. When she was satisfied, she put the knife on the dresser and pulled a chair up. Simfany pulled away the wool fabric; the two black duffle bags she put there almost a year earlier still remained intact. She grabbed both bags and sat them at her feet. Simfany opened the one closest to her. When she opened it, she realized it was the bag that contained the money and guns that she took out of Emilio's safe. The other duffle bag was the money Byrd gave her for the eight bricks he flipped.

The little fortune wasn't worth the problems it caused. Simfany took the money from the bricks and put it with Emilio's stash money. Before she closed the bag, Simfany walked over to the dresser and grabbed the box of bullets, also putting them in the bag. She struggled as she tried her best to move the mattress back into its place. *Fuck it*, she told herself, letting the mat fall on top of the box spring awkwardly. She gathered the things she came for and left the house; this time, gun in hand.

Jamel Mitchell

Chapter Two

The week was almost at its end and Blaze still didn't turn up to Mandella Hall. Santana and Drew were getting impatient; they were tired of waiting on him. Santana tried to keep Drew occupied so he wouldn't stress, but Santana found himself most of the time alone or talking to various lames. Rolando was also housed on Mandella Hall, so at times Santana kicked it with him when Drew was in one of his modes. There was peace on unit 1 but it was boring. The days seemed as if they were getting longer to him. The only way he seemed to get away was when he worked in the kitchen on the unit. The best thing about the job was you ate good, you actually got to be comfortable and relax, and they got the chance to rap with the cute kitchen workers. Rolando worked with Santana in the kitchen. Santana and Rolando clicked well. Rolando wasn't the same person he met only months ago when he found out the news about Simfany, while he was in segregation. He was actually the opposite. Rolando was fairly quiet and kept to himself, but what everybody did know about Rolando was he'd live and die for the sake of the five. That was one of the reasons Santana took a liking to him. He seemed to learn a lot from him. Santana just hoped he wouldn't have to ruin a friendship over what he and Drew planned on doing to the nigga Blaze. Blaze was also known in Hickey to get down for his bandana. His loyalty was with Tijuana, so he never second guessed any decisions he made regarding her. Homie or no homie, when it was reppin' time, he knew who he was riding with: *Tijuana Moore*. That name spoke louder than any color. This was what Blaze thought about as he relaxed on a milk crate in the little kitchen.

"What's poppin' lor yo? You spaced out." Rolando said as he wiped the sink.

"Got a lot on my mind, my G," Santana replied.

"It's noticeable. The only advice I could give you is keep ya head up, shorty." Rolando finished cleaning, giving Santana his space. Rolando knew what it felt like to be a young nigga locked up. Especially when you had a family that loved you.

"Rolando, keep it all the way real with me, how do you feel about ya homies?"

"Meaning what?" Rolando stopped wiping down the counter to pay attention to Santana.

"I mean, like, niggas from different hoods and shit. I just been curious because I see a lot of niggas walking 'round here and they damu, but you stay clear of them. What I'm asking is why?" Santana asked curiously.

"Let me put it to you like this, lor yo, every blood is not your blood. We war with ourselves more than we war with the people we call our *enemies*. The game is turning into a fashion show and it's breeding all these lame ass niggas. Just because they pop the five don't mean it's a must that I break bread with them. I would love to, though. It's just sad that the love isn't right but look how these niggas run around here. Don't get me wrong. Till my death date I will acknowledge blood because of the niggas that did this shit before us, but if I'm not needed I'm cool. You feel me?" Rolando explained.

"Yeah, I can feel that son."

"You an alright lor nigga, so the day you decide what you want to do or who you think you must become, make sure your big homie a real nigga. You are an image of ya superior. So, if he a bitch nigga, then no disrespect, but you gone be a bitch nigga—so be careful. You'd be surprised at the misleading of this shit. So please be wise."

"Good looking, my nigga, I'm definitely not trying to be misled," Santana said with pride.

"It's easy, be yourself. You don't need to try when you have it in ya heart. Not all the time, but real niggas make it, homie. Always remember, lor nigga: *Hard times don 't last, real niggas do.* Now pick your head up before Nicki have a fit when she comes back." He threw Santana the rag he was using. Santana got the hint and started to wipe down the burners. The rest of the night went without incident.

The day began like many others, Santana taking his shower and getting his hygiene in order. He usually went undisturbed because of the hour he chose. Today somebody was in the bathroom with him, a new face. Santana stepped under one of the six shower heads and took a quick shower. Santana was still in a state of slumber that he didn't pay attention to the other person's face. Plus, it was an unspoken rule not to talk while you were in the shower. So, he kept his head up, washed and exited the shower.

Santana got out the shower and got dressed. He was at the sink when he finally got the chance to see the boy's face. Santana hadn't ever seen the boy before, so he dismissed him automatically. He continued to get himself right. The dark-skinned kid took the sink right next to Santana, so it made him look over. The kid nodded. Santana nodded back. Santana grabbed his belongings and left the bathroom. As he was leaving, Bumpy came in. Before Santana got out of earshot, he thought he heard the name Blaze come out of Bumpy's mouth. *Nah, I'm tripping*, Santana told himself as he continued back to his cell. Geezy was making his bed when Santana got back to his room. Santana finished combing his hair, but he couldn't shake the thought of Bumpy saying Blaze's name.

"What's good, shorty? Nigga, you be up early in this bitch," Geezy said as he put on his grey sweats and a fresh white tee, daily Hickey attire.

"Gotta get my mind right, son, you know how shit is," Santana replied, fixing his bed.

"You been to the bathroom yet?" Santana asked.

"Nah, why, what's up?" Geezy asked suspiciously.

"Some new nigga came in and he look familiar, and I ain't got time for the drama. But I'm not sure it is who I think it is. You'd know if he was on Clinton Hall with me," Santana told him.

"I got you, lor yo, I'm 'bout to go see about this nigga right now," Geezy said as he walked out of the room. Santana waited for Glen to come back. Geezy returned within five minutes.

"Are you talking 'bout the dark-skinned nigga?" Geezy asked.

"Yeah, he looks familiar, doesn't he? I can't place the face though." Santana looked like he was clueless. It was amusing to him. But he didn't want to be obvious and ask straight out about Blaze. Santana didn't know who was riding with Blaze, so he played his cards to the best of his ability.

"Nah, he wasn't on Clinton Hall when you were there. He just got booked for a body. That's the nigga Blaze. He from the county. Ya man Drew should know him," Geezy said in a matter-of-fact tone.

"Good looking," Santana said as he began to lace up his shoes. He tried to conceal his anxiety, but he couldn't. Geezy sat on his bed and watched Santana get war-ready. Geezy sensed the anger that Santana tried his best to disguise.

"Tana, you good, lor yo?"

"Yeah, why, what's up?"

"My nigga, you acting funny right now. You breathing all hard, you zoned out." Glen looked at Santana.

"Nah, my G, I'm good. Word to my mom's!" Santana said and walked out the room.

Santana walked to Drew's room and knocked on the door. Drew spaced out yet again. *Man, this nigga losing his marbles*, Santana thought as he opened the door.

"Big homie," Santana called out. Drew was still looking at the window.

"Drew!" Santana called louder. This time it caught Drew's attention and Santana could tell that he was irritated. Drew's gaze lightened when he saw Santana in the doorway.

"Oh, shit, my bad, shorty. What's good for real?" Drew walked over to Santana.

"That nigga Blaze here on God." The look in Drew's eyes told it all.

"You sure?" Drew asked as he started to strap his shoes up.

"No, I don't know for real, but my bunkie said it was him. Shit, your Bumpy was the one I seen greet the nigga earlier. I thought he said Blaze name. That's why I had Geezy go out and find out for me." Santana explained the events of that morning.

"A'ight, let's go show shorty how we rock," Drew said as he pulled the razor from a spot under his bed. C.O. Green gave Drew the razor the week prior for an unrelated reason, but Drew kept the tool for this purpose.

"Look, Tana, you crack the nigga and I'm gone eat this nigga."

"I got you," Santana answered. The pair started to walk out the room but was stopped when Drew turned and looked Santana in his face. He saw fear, but Drew understood it was natural.

"Shorty, I got this nigga by myself, you ain't got to go. Regardless, you my nigga, so don't do this for me. I'm good." Drew reassured him, yet Santana's face scrunched up as he looked at Drew.

"Fuck I look like, nigga? Loyalty is everything, remember!" Santana replied proudly. Santana knew that his eyes told the story of his anxiousness, but he wasn't scared.

"You right." Drew smiled.

"Wait on me. I'm gone go see what cell the nigga live in." Santana walked down the hall nonchalantly, looking into all the cells for Blaze. Fortunately for them, Blaze was in the last cell in the back. It would be that door in the back that would later save Blaze's life, though. After he found the cell Blaze stayed in, Santana made his way back to Drew's cell.

"Blaze in the last cell to the right. He was sitting down with his head in his hands."

"Let's go," Drew said as he led the way down the hallway. Each step Santana took, he became more and more anxious. Knowing that blood was about to be shed excited him, but he was nervous all in the same breath. Santana surely didn't want to kill nobody. *But fuck it,* he thought. *It's all about loyalty, right?* That single word—*Loyalty*—would eventually become Santana's friend and foe. Santana no longer questioned his actions; it was reppin' time. Santana stopped Drew by pulling his shirt.

"I'm gone get him out his room and we gone smash the nigga for ya man and Tijuana."

"You cool with that?" Santana asked. Drew nodded. He walked to the cell door and peeked in.

"Breakfast, homie," Santana told Blaze as he posted outside of his door. When Santana saw a glimpse of Blaze, he swung. Caught off guard, Blaze rolled with the punch and caught Santana twice in the face. Santana dropped instantly off the impact of the punches. Blaze looked down at Santana; he didn't see Drew hiding in the room across from him. When Drew saw Santana get dropped, he ran out and caught Blaze with a swift left hook, stumbling him back into his room and away from Santana.

Drew swung the blade connecting with Blaze's shoulder, opening him up badly. After the, first sign of blood, Drew swung again. Blaze weaved the second attempt and shot a jab at Drew, dropping him on impact. Blaze then rushed Drew, punishing him on the ground. Santana, still dazed from the hit, got up and swung with all his might, connecting with the side of Blaze's head. Blaze hit the wall near the window. The punch didn't knock him out, but it dazed him long enough for Santana to kick Blaze in his head. *That'll sit him on his ass,* Santana encouraged himself. Drew got up and pushed Santana out of the room.

"Go, lor nigga!" Drew yelled.

"Nah, son, let's go," Santana said as he tried to run past Drew.

"Lor yo, go! Please. You handled you!" Drew pleaded. Santana turned around and took off out of the room. As he jogged down the hall, he heard someone yell. He didn't want to go back; he just hoped it was the voice of that coward nigga Blaze. He had made it back to his room by the time C.O. Green came in the back. Santana caught eye contact with Green and nodded. Santana nodded down the hall. Green took off; he hoped he was in time. Santana watched on as Green and Drew came out the cell. Green waited until Drew was down the hall before he called in for assistance.

"Staff support! Staff support—Mandella Hall. Bring medical, this dude looks like he 'bout to die!" Green yelled into his walkie talkie. "Staff support—Mandella Hall!" Drew walked up to Santana and hugged him.

"I love you for this, shorty," Drew said.

"Likewise, my nigga, but go change your clothes before the rest of the C.O.'s come, and throw that shit away, nigga. You trippin'." Santana pointed at the bloody blade.

"A'ight." Drew rushed into his cell and changed into clean clothes; Santana did the same. Santana took the clothes from Drew and walked them to the laundry cart near the bathroom, and buried them inside the basket. He went undetected because of all the confusion. After he buried the clothes deep enough, he walked back to his cell as if nothing happened. When Santana bent the corner, Drew was in a heated argument with his bunkie—a light-skinned skinny cat everyone knew as Bumpy. Him and Drew locked eyes. Santana approached at a slow pace. Bumpy was being extremely animated with his hands. Knowing Drew and how he rocked, he would probably have felt threatened by the hand motions. Drew shook his head, trying to explain, then Drew looked down. Santana could tell he was aggravated. Santana looked on. Bumpy took the look Drew gave as a sign defeat. Santana watched as Drew looked up at him then at Bumpy, but Bumpy was so caught up in being tough he didn't pay attention to his opponent. That was a mistake on Bumpy's part. Drew didn't hesitate. Drew stole off on Bumpy. Santana wasted no time in running over, jumping in. Bumpy tried to go blow for blow with Drew, but when Santana caught him from the back, it took all the fight out of him. Bumpy tried to turn and look back, but his chin was met with yet another right hook dazing him. Drew knocked him out with the next hit. Bumpy hit the floor hard. Santana and Drew started to stomp him with everything they had. Santana stopped kicking when his leg started to cramp. Bumpy was curled in the fetal position and now fully awake. Santana grabbed Drew.

"Come on, nigga," Santana pulled until Drew finally walked off with him. They looked down the hall as transportation and medical tried to help Blaze out the back door, the one closest to his room. For the first time in about a week, Santana saw a smile on Drew's face. Drew looked down at the light-skinned kid Santana only knew as Bumpy, and spat on him. "Next time, mind your business, pussy." Santana looked at Bumpy and felt bad. He didn't know what took place while he was at the laundry cart, and he would never ask. It didn't matter. So, he left it at that. Santana looked up at the confusion they caused on Mandella Hall. Santana didn't want it to get out of control, but as long as Blaze got smashed, nothing else mattered. He just hoped it made Tijuana feel a little better. "Lockdown!" Mr. Underwood yelled from the intersection of the hallway. Bumpy laid on the floor, trying to regain himself.

"Lock the fuck down!" The hallway was now full of C.O.'s from all over the jail. Transportation officers were everywhere, in the instant that someone felt too tough and bucked.

Santana made eye contact with C.O. Green before he closed his door. He knew Green would pass on the message to Tijuana about what happened. Satisfied, Santana closed the door and locked in. Glen paced back and forth in the cell.

"Lor yo, y'all niggas is crazy," Glen said excitedly.

"Nah, my G. It's consequences to every action. It ain't shit, the nigga will be a'ight." Santana laughed; he found the whole situation funny. He knew it would all catch up to him one day, but while he had the upper hand, he promised himself to take advantage of it. Glen knew Santana was too far gone on excitement, but in all truth he was too. The situation that took place rarely happened on Mandella. It would bring order back, restoring Mandella into a relatively calm unit.

***

Santana went to sleep that night knowing that a six-to-nine-month sentence might be too far out of arms reach, especially after the events of the day. He was in too deep. The love he had for his niggas would always override the conscious decisions he would make in life. As he lay, Santana slowly began to evolve into a man each day that passed. The innocence he once possessed was no longer there. The one word in life that meant the most to Santana would one day eventually get him killed. He called it *being loyal by default*, whereas it was a beginning only to a critical ending.

Drew was pulled out later that day and was questioned by the state police regarding his involvement in the attempt to murder Narvel "Blaze" Harris. Santana was also questioned about the incident. Both men denied involvement. They even denied knowing Blaze. The six-to-nine-month program seemed to be slipping away as each day passed. Santana knew his lawyer would be upset if the deal was taken off of the table, but it was nothing he could do. What was done was done.

Rick Holliver didn't feel that way at all. When he heard about the type of shit going on in Hickey regarding Santana, he lost his nerve for a second. *This boy won 't be any different than the rest,* he thought as he made the emergency drive to Hickey to see what was going on.

Santana walked into the gym and saw his lawyer seated at the far right waiting for him. The expression he had on his face told it all. He was pissed. *Fuck this nigga*, Santana thought as he made his way to the awaiting chair. Rick didn't stand to greet Santana; he just stared at him.

"What's up?" Santana asked as he took his seat. He was ready to play the game.

"You tell me, what are you doing? You just got your plea a week ago. What is going on?" Mr. Holliver asked.

"Shit happens." Santana answered.

"Well, you tell that lame ass comment to your mother when you don't come home until you're grown. Don't get caught up in the lure. This is not a place you want to be or grow up in!" Mr. Holliver explained to Santana. Santana nodded in agreement.

"I feel you, but some things happen."

"I do understand that, but you and Mr. Henry tried to kill Narvel Harris. I'm not going to ask why or what part you played, but I will tell you this—you're stupid. Do your time and go home to your mother. She needs you more than these niggas in Hickey co. I grew up around a lot of these same people but I made it out because I fought against adversity. Now look at me, one of the best lawyers the city has seen in a long time. It's not hard, Santana. Anyway, I came here to let you know Mr. Harris didn't press any charges, so again you got God on your side. Now that doesn't mean Ms. Price can't take your plea back, because she can and in all truth she might. My job is to fight for you. But my question is, are you gone fight for yourself? And I don't mean in the literal sense." Rick looked at the papers he held in his hands. Santana thought about what his lawyer said, but he didn't regret what he did. Rick looked up; he recognized the look in Santana's eyes. The boy was no longer an innocent 13-year-old caught up in his circumstances.

Santana's innocence was long gone. There was nothing left. It was sad, because the reality of being a young black man in a fucked-up community always outweighed the good. Rick knew this wouldn't be the last time he had to represent Santana. He cared about his community, but if people wanted to continue to break the law and pay him, so be it.

"This, what I'm going to do, in the next couple of days I'm going to go and talk to Ms. Price myself about this *misunderstanding.* If she let you keep this plea, you know what you have to do. Stay out of trouble if you want to go home. It's your choice, Santana. Don't be a statistic."

"I got you, but understand I got to survive. And to survive I can't show any signs of weakness. The first time you do, that's when shit get extremely hard. So, I'll try my hardest."

"I hear you. It's your life on the line, not mine. Do what needs to be done and go home."

"Okay," Santana replied. Mr. Holliver packed his belongings and left. He left with the disappointment buried deep. He had a better vision for Santana than all this street shit. He saw Santana as a bright kid that was placed in a fucked-up circumstance. Rick couldn't fault him for the decision he made. Santana protected his mother the only way he knew how at the time. Rick respected that. What he saw was an innocent misguided child who really needed help. And that help wouldn't come from the other kids in Hickey, if he could help it.

Rick Holliver hopped in his car. He put away his paperwork and looked in the mirror. *You made it,* he told himself proudly as he stroked his goatee. He pulled out of the parking lot of the Charles H. Hickey School for boys in hopes of keeping Santana's plea deal active.

Chapter Three

Simfany had just got off the phone with Santana's lawyer, Rick Holliver. He explained to her the situation that he currently had on his hands. At first the news had her feeling some kind of way, but she couldn't blame anybody but herself. She was the reason behind it all. After her meeting with Carlos, she decided to have a sit-down with Santana to explain everything. She wanted him to know everything; it was time to stop bullshitting. Meanwhile, in Judge Price's chambers, Rick was again fighting for his client.

"Your honor, my client is a scared child that is very small. He has to protect himself," Rick explained.

"That's okay and understandable, but he and another boy almost killed that Narvel kid. Not only is he cut bad, but he's a primary witness in a murder case." Rick looked puzzled. He did research on Blaze, but that popped up nowhere.

"What do you mean he's a state witness?" he asked confusingly.

"A child by the name of Kane Moore was gunned down in Harford County about a week ago, leaving Narvel Harris as the prime suspect, a known blood member in a Crip neighborhood. In a turn of events a family killed one of their own. Andre Jones was a Crip and he was the gun man. Mr. Harris gave a complete statement and agreed to testify to clear his own butt. And now you're telling me that the client you represent was a part of an attempt on his life. Am I right?" Rick nodded.

"Yes, ma'am."

"Why shouldn't I take back Mr. Vasquez's plea deal? It seems like he doesn't want to go home. It hasn't been a month since I've sentenced him and yet you're here trying to keep his plea intact. So again, why should I let him keep his plea, Mr. Holliver?" Judge Price asked from the other side of her desk with a stern look on her face.

"Honestly, for more reasons than one. The boy is extremely young, scared and easy influenced. Plus his mother is having problems of her own. He wasn't charged with any new crimes. I really believe that when this child gets out, the street life won't be a problem for him." Rick answered, not believing his own words.

"Look, I'm going to leave the agreement as it stands, but and I mean *but,* if Mr. Vasquez catches any new charges or cannot complete a program, he will do juvenile life. So please pass that on to him. There's no room for error."

"Thank you, your honor. You have a blessed day." Rick smiled as he gathered his belongings.

"You keep that boy out of trouble, Rick."

"Okay, I will." Rick left Judge Price's chambers feeling like a million dollars. He played his part. Now it was up to Santana to play his. Two weeks passed by before Tijuana came back to work. The gleam she once had was dim. The death of her brother took a lot out of her; she wanted answers. But nobody seemed willing to give her any explanation. The detective working the case wouldn't even tell her much.

The word traveled fast that Blaze was going to testify on Dre. Nobody respected that way out, especially when you were a character in a game for keeps. The most disappointed was the niggas Blaze called family. None of that mattered to Tijuana; all she wanted was revenge. Tijuana was too deep in thought; she didn't hear Santana come into the office.

"Yo, ma, what's poppin'?" He looked concerned. Tijuana looked up, pushing her thoughts aside.

"What's up, baby boy? How you been doing?" she asked.

"Those are the questions I'm supposed to be asking you. I need big sis back. I know your brother died and I swear my heart truly goes out to you, but it's time to get yourself back together. He wouldn't want to see you fucked up like this. It's not wrong to miss him. That was your baby brother, but ma, handle it the way he would. Try at least." Tijuana just listened.

"You don't understand, Santana," she whispered.

"Then help me understand, Tijuana. I'm a young nigga, but I'm far from dumb. Explain to me what's on ya mind."

"My brother was a good nigga, but he had flaws. Everyone does, but he was a good person, at least to the people that mattered anyway. I think what hurts more is to think about the nigga that ended his life. These two niggas grew up wearing *Power Ranger* pj's. Kane and Dre were best friends when they were growing up. That alone should be enough for the problem to be avoided, especially over a nigga like Blaze. I don't know my lor nigga lost his life over some bullshit." Tijuana cried. Santana didn't know what it felt like to lose somebody so close. He was fucked up over his mother when she was shot, so he could only imagine. He couldn't fathom losing his mother. Just the thought made him grab Tijuana and hug her tightly, hoping the tears would stop.

"Look, ma, I know I can't replace your brother, but you know you got a lil' brother in me. And I'm gone be here for you as long as you need me to."

"I know you will. That's why I fuck with you. How Drew holding up? I been trying to avoid talking to y'all because my moods haven't been the best, plus they got me under investigation." Tijuana laughed. Santana knew she was talking about the situation with Blaze. He thought of Blaze.

"Fuck that nigga. He couldn't hold water for a nigga that killed for him, no disrespect ma, I know he gone tell on *us*. Fuck it though. It's what I signed up for. I love you, T, and I fucks with you hard, so I'm gone be around regardless whether the police investigating or not. You're my baby." He laughed at his own sarcasm. She finally smiled.

"I feel you."

"But for real, ma, you got to keep ya head up, especially around these niggas. They thrive off of your downfall. But for you, me and Drew will fall back until the investigation is over with. I would hate to lose you. Just promise to keep ya head up, and know we love you ma."

"I promise. Things will be back to normal soon hopefully. Thank you for all that you do. You're appreciated," Tijuana replied softly. Santana hugged Tijuana again before he departed.

***

"Ramos, I'm telling you; I witnessed this muthafuckin meeting. Somehow Simfany Vasquez is connected to Carlos Rivera!" Detective Lawson tried to explain.

"Lawson, the only connection would be Byrd. Byrd worked for Carlos for years as his henchman. Baltimore in a whole was scared of the duo!" Detective Ramos shot back.

"So, by the way of your attitude, you're telling me this isn't a big break?" Lawson looked at Ramos crazily.

"It depends. The reason I say that is because the only way this can be big is if you can put some meaning to that meeting between the two. Let me see—" Ramos rubbed his chin and looked up to the ceiling as if he was thinking extremely hard about something. Ramos continued:

"Alright, let me ask this, why was the meeting important? Can you answer that? Besides, the two people that was there, where does the importance lie?" Lawson said nothing because he only was going off his gut feeling.

"That's my point exactly," Ramos said before he went back to typing on his computer.

"The word on the street was: Carlos was the one that got Simfany hit. And if true, why go through the hassle of meeting up? It makes no sense." Before he could catch himself, he realized what he said when he said it. Ramos looked at Lawson with that knowing glance.

"Look, I'm not telling you to go with ya gut. It's fishy and it raises an eyebrow or two. But it's not big because of Byrd being the connection between the two. Now if for any reason you don't think they knew each other before his death, then that would be something *big*. Before you get too sidetracked, I think you should be looking into the little brother. The hot line is on fire and he's the main topic. A lot of people think he killed his brother!" Ramos explained.

"No, I can't see that. Look at it this way—Big brother is a legend, why would you kill him? He's family! That really doesn't add up. That's more farfetched than my theory about Carlos and Simfany." Lawson was getting irritated with his partner. Ramos looked up from his computer.

"Not really everybody has their own story on why they believe Jimdog to be his killer. There was one story that did stand out and make a lot of sense to me. They said Jimdog lived in his brother's shadow for too long. Nobody looked at Jimdog to be an outright soldier until after his first bid in Juvey. And even after he did what he did, he was still Byrd's little brother. A lot of the older cats treated him according to how they treated his brother. Jimdog was feared because of his brother. Nobody wanted to go against Byrd. Jimdog got tired of the fame his brother produced on his behalf. He sought out for his own. Of course, there are many ways he could have gone about it, but he felt killing his brother was the best way out. He murdered probably one of the only people that loved him for him. That's what was told to me, and to be honest whether it's hundred percent accurate or not, I believe that can be the closest we may come." Lawson looked at his partner and busted out laughing. What Ramos said tickled him.

"Fuck is so funny?" Ramos moved from in front of his computer.

"Nothing, partner," Lawrence replied. "Sometimes you just kill me. You're one track minded. If you're settled on a theory that's what you're fixed on. Nobody else's opinion counts, because all jokes aside—seeing Simfany Vasquez and Carlos Rivera together at the wee hours of the morning is more important than a caller with some story. I'm not like you. I won't take that out of the equation, it gives me something else to connect to my theory."

"How about you follow your leads and I follow mine? Whoever gets closest wins gets dinner anywhere in the city." Detective Ramos put out his fist to seal the deal. Lawson gladly agreed. Both men were close to knowing the importance of their cases, just in their own little way.

As Simfany drove down Cub Hill Road in Baltimore County, she thought about the chances she had of losing her only child to the secrets she held. Today was the day she would tell Santana the story from beginning to present. Simfany drove and thought about how both their lives changed in a matter of six months. The Charles

H. Hickey School for boys sat at the end of the 2400 block of Cub Hill Road.

Simfany was granted access to the visitation area. She picked her normal seat she always picked when she came to see Santana, a set of chairs that was off into the comer away from everybody. She took her seat and waited on her son to arrive. Ten minutes passed before Santana finally showed up in the gym. Simfany watched Santana's every move. She began to cry. *My baby is getting so big,* she thought as he walked over to her. No matter how much he grew, he would still be her little baby boy. Simfany hugged Santana tight. She missed him badly. She could tell he missed her just as much. Their love was one of a kind.

"I love you, baby boy," Simfany said, still in an embrace.

"I love you too, mommy," Santana replied. They both took their seats.

"So, what's the pleasure of you coming earlier than expected?" Santana asked jokingly.

"Just wanted to see my son. Is there a problem with that?" she joked back.

"I was just saying."

"I know but on a serious note—I did come to talk to you about some important things." Simfany got serious.

"Man, I hope Rick ain't telling you no bullshit." Santana was nervous. Simfany had forgotten about the conversation she had with her lawyer. She would speak her peace on the situation, that was for sure.

"I know all about the dude Blaze. I'm going to keep my comments to myself right now.

This conversation me and you need to have will remain between us do you hear me?" she said with seriousness in her tone. Santana nodded in agreement, realizing the severity of the conversation. Simfany began telling her story.

"Everything I do, I do for our family. Okay, let me explain a little more. Remember Emilio my boyfriend?" she asked, making sure she had his full attention.

"Yes. You talking 'bout the nigga that killed my father!" he said aggressively.

"Yeah, well, Emilio got a lot of money with your father. They were raised from papers together. Ya dad thought about stepping away from the game because you were on the way. He told Emilio that he would be the next to take Melrose over. So, Emilio waited patiently—"

"I'm not trying to hear about the nigga that killed my father!" Santana glared at his mother.

"Who the fuck is you yelling at, nigga? Listen to what the fuck I have to say. So, like I was saying, Emilio waited patiently. Your father changed his mind after you was born and stayed planted feet first. Emilio grew jealous of your father. At your first birthday, Emilio decided to take your father's life. I watched the love of my life die in front of my eyes. It was so—" Santana cut her off yet again.

"It couldn't have been that bad. You were messing with Emilio after that." Simfany took the blow on the chin and continued as if he never interrupted.

"I used all the money your father left to raise you and bought the club. After your father was killed, I continued to run into Emilio on a regular basis. I couldn't take seeing him live life no more, so I formulated a plan. I know this is not something you want to hear, but what I possess between my legs make niggas weak-minded and stupid, Emilio being the prime victim. I put time in with the nigga. I got all his combinations to safes and I earned his trust. So, one night I waited for him to come home and I smoked him, taking *everything,* he owned. Duffle bags full of money, drugs and guns." Santana looked at his mother. Before he could interrupt again, she answered his question. "No, I didn't kill him for the money. That was a bonus. I killed that nigga because he took your father away from us. That was the reason I wanted to leave New York and start somewhere else. That turned out to be the worst decision I ever made. After I left you with Lonnie, I came to Baltimore and met a man by the name of Byrd. Not on that kind of tip." She lied. "He was a real nigga that had a lot of respect. We met at a club. We became best friends, almost. He was a cool person, and I began to actually trust him. His loyalty ran deep. I came to Baltimore with eight bricks of cocaine. I had Byrd sell the drugs for me at a low price. Byrd gave me my cut of the split and went back and flipped again for himself. He stayed in business for himself. Oh, I forgot to mention Byrd was a henchman that worked for a drug boss named Carlos. Crazy, huh? This the type of shit you only see in a movie. I thought so at least. Anyway, Byrd went to the county to get money, but unknowingly he was still on Carlos's territory. Even though that was Byrd's boss, he was also his mentor. Carlos and Byrd couldn't come to an understanding regarding the territory, so they started a war. The war didn't last long because the two men had too much of a profound love for each other. Byrd continued to do his thing but later came up missing. At first, I thought Carlos had him killed, but I just spoke to Carlos a couple of nights ago and he said he had nothing to do with Byrd's death. He being a man with his kind of power, you tend to believe—" Santana cut her off.

"So where do we come in at?"

"I'm not done. This shit seems like it never ends. Jimdog came home from Hickey during all of this and he wanted to know what happened to his brother. At first it was all love between us, and then out the blue he started taking shots at me as if I killed Byrd, or that I knew about it. But I didn't. This body had nothing to do with me. Byrd was found floating in the harbor. Jimdog came at me hard, but I stopped seeing him, so I thought he was done tripping. That's where you came down here and we went to that damn picnic at Druid Hill Park. The rest is history. The only thing that bothers me is not knowing who shot me and why. Jimdog didn't know where I stayed at, so it's confusing."

"What about the dude Carlos?" Santana asked.

"I just had a meeting with him, and he said he was here to protect us. He knew somebody your father knew. So, he feels obligated, I guess, to help. But we don't need the nigga. As long as he not the one shooting, then we good. I don't think he sent nobody to kill me. It was a blue flag, nigga, that's all I know." She seemed clueless.

"What other niggas was Byrd fucking with besides Carlos?" Santana asked.

"Some blood dudes from Harford County," she answered. Santana grew silent.

"Did you say Harford County? Don't you live in Harford County with Carol?"

"Yeah, so what? Them niggas don't know me. Byrd wasn't that kind of nigga, Tana. He was very loyal." Santana wasn't convinced at all. It was too much of a coincidence.

"What gang were they a part of?" he asked.

"Boy, I don't know." Simfany started to get annoyed about the whole situation.

"If I was to say the name of the gang, would you remember?"

"Yeah, most likely, I only remember little about them. Never seen any of them before so I wouldn't know what they looked like either. But—" Santana cut in.

"TTP or Tree Top Piru, does that ring a bell?" Santana asked as if the set popped into his mind that second. Simfany's face turned red, and her palms got sweaty.

"Yeah! That's the set of niggas that was eating with Byrd. How you know about them?" Santana leaned in toward his mother.

"My nigga tried to kill one of them niggas the other day," he whispered, leaving himself out of the equation altogether.

"Oh, that's the Blaze dude you almost got in trouble over?" Simfany was puzzled. She didn't understand how it all fit together, but it did.

"So, what do you make of this big ass coincidence?" Simfany asked Santana.

"I don't know, but something told me to ask you about them niggas. But that's where the road ends. I don't know shit about them dudes. I just know Blaze is TTP and he's from the county where that dude Byrd was getting money." "Now that I said what's been going on since you popped out, how do you feel?" Santana could see the worried look on her face as she finished her last statement. He laughed.

"Timeout, you came here thinking I would be mad at you after you told me all ya secrets? You trippin', ma. You're my mother. I'm here to protect you also. What we go through, we go through together. You bleed, I bleed. Unless you put a slug in me yourself, I could never hate or be mad at you. You're all I have and that's enough for me. I love you, pretty lady. My loyalty is with you forever. For real, ma, I don't care what type of beef or issues you may get into, I inherit that beef by blood. I can tell you one thing though; you are a trip." He laughed yet again at his mother. Behind the smile he felt as if he was dying inside. It killed him that she hid all that from him. He didn't want her to worry too much, so he kept it to himself. Simfany had looked bad enough. At the end of the day, he would get over it as if it never happened.

"I love you, Santana. Mommy won't keep any more secrets. Please stay out of trouble. I need you out there with me. Six months ain't shit. Come home."

"Visitation hours are over in five minutes!" a C.O. called out from the front of the gym's entrance.

"I love you too. I'm glad you told me everything. I got a better understanding now.

Remember what I said. Don't be snooping around to find answers. I'll see what's what when I get home. Give me a kiss." Santana grabbed his favorite person in the world and held on to her as if he would never get the chance to hold her again.

"I love you, pretty lady."

"I love you too, Santana, baby, please stay out of trouble."

"You got it," Santana replied. Simfany made her way out with the rest of the visitors, leaving Santana alone with his thoughts.

It was a mercury afternoon as Santana rode back to Mandella Hall. The day couldn't get any better, but with his luck it would get worse. The tension on the pod was at a minimum. Nobody was really beefing with nobody. People who didn't like each other remained cordial.

Tijuana started to come back a little from the death of her brother, and it showed through the attitude of the inmates housed in Mandella.

"What's poppin, homie? How you feeling today?" Rolando asked him.

"I'm good, five, my mom just came up here to see me and you know it was good to see my lady," Santana answered while they started to set up in the kitchen, awaiting the food truck.

"I seen you and lor youngin' Drew been falling back. Shit 'bout time. You lor niggas are crazy. Don't see too many that's ready to go. Especially at a young age, that's why I fuck with you. By the way, what's good with ya red ruby you use to spit about, she still riding?" Rolando asked.

"Yeah, it's here and there, you know how they get." Santana shrugged.

"Nah, shorty. She got a life to live, my dude. Your fuck up, not hers. If you wanna get back to her, you gotta chill. Six months all you got for real. So, fall back," Rolando said as he put the burners on to the heat up the food. After dinner was over, Santana went in his room and analyzed his life. It was a good one so far, minus the new bullshit. He made a pact within himself to find out about them TTP niggas and whether they had something to do with Simfany's shooting, because until he knew the answers, he wouldn't be able to rest.

Jamel Mitchell

Chapter Four

On the streets of Edgewood Blaze's name buzzed with a fucked-up certainty. Once known to the streets as a goon, now turned rat. The image was a bad one, one that could get you killed for. The ones hurt most behind the situation was Hood Ru and Stacks. The three grew up together and were close like brothers. Watching all the drama unfold was like a bad movie. It didn't seem real to the pair. The nick name Blaze came from Narvel putting in work as a youngin'.

As both men sat in Hood's Cherry Red 1996 bubble Caprice, they read the statement Blaze gave to the detectives. Each word that they read broke their hearts. What they couldn't understand was *why*. Why tell now? That was the real question. Blaze knew the knowledge of a couple murders that went unsolved. Yet he didn't tell that. It really did not make sense. What did make sense was that Blaze was no longer welcomed in Harford Commons. Birds of a feather flock together; understanding that kind of terminology, Blaze was food if seen in the "Commons".

"Damn, Ru, this nigga straight ratted on Bull," Hood said in his Philly accent.

"I can read, my nigga, but what we gone do if the nigga try to slide back through here?" Stacks asked Hood as he leaned in his back seat.

"Nigga, you know what we gone do. We gone sick one of them young bulls on him. I got too much time and love with the nigga to rock him to sleep myself," Hood explained.

"I do too, but shorty broke the code we as a whole are all against. I feel you though. Shorty was like a lor brother to me. He can live anywhere but in this city. If he comes back, he wants to die. So, you tell them niggas if they see shorty anywhere in our city—smoke him. Tell all the stain-chasing niggas, I said rank come with his head if he is seen out here!" Stacks said as he looked out the window of the Caprice.

This nigga drawn for real, Hood thought to himself.

"I got you, but other than that you know shorty just moved to Meadowood, right?" Hood said, breaking his train of thought.

"What shorty? Shorty you met at Hammer Jacks?" Stacks wondered.

"Nah, the cute Rican bitch that fucked with the bull Byrd," Hood explained.

"Oh, you talking about Simfany or Sophia, whatever her name is?" Stacks replied.

"Yeah. What's up with her? She a red dot or what?" Hood raised up and looked at his brethren.

"Nah, she straight. The message came down the line to leave her be. Carlos is willing to go to war over her." Stacks laughed and shrugged. Hood's face was that of confusion.

"I know. I don't get it either. But fuck it. She straight in my book with her sexy ass," Stacks admitted. Hood looked at Stacks and smiled. *That's because you 're the one that shot her with ya nut ass,* Hood thought. For the rest of the day the pair just chilled, smoked and read Blaze's paperwork over and over. The disappointment turned to angry lingering thoughts. Each mind held its own demons about Narvel Harris that neither was willing to admit.

Nine Months Later—*Backbone Mountain School (MD)*

"You a bitch, son. But you got it, my nigga. I don't want no smoke. You Greenmount niggas too tough for me." Santana laughed at Daron once again. Daron stood, trying to intimidate Santana. Standing at 5'10 and Santana at 5'3, the difference didn't matter. The outcome would be the outcome.

"Lor shorty, I'll smash you. But you lucky I'm trying to make it home," Daron replied with a mean mug attached to his face. The beef between Santana and Daron started off when they first. Daron felt Santana was handed shit in life, not knowing what the boy been through. Santana recognized shade from the beginning and played his distance. Many times, Santana bumped heads with Daron. The only thing that kept Santana calm was Rolando. Rolando was trans-ferred to Backbone months back. But the two were on different groups, so they could barely talk.

When Santana got out of control, Rolando gave him a look to chill, because he wouldn't be the only one in trouble if shit got real. Santana respected the love and played his cards wisely. With going home on his mind, he tried to let a lot of things ride. Yet, he was pushed on a daily basis. Santana was now fourteen years old but was soon to be fifteen. He grew a lot mentally but he never tolerated disrespect. He had a motto he lived by: *You let 'em slide once, that's when the losing start.* Even though his mother didn't agree with his decisions, she understood. It was going on a year since Santana first got booked. He couldn't complete any programs that were given to him because of his behavior. The only good thing for Santana was: Jimdog stopped coming to the court hearings. Judge Price took ju-venile life off the table, but Santana still had to complete a six-to-nine-month program.

"So, what's good then, son?" Santana advanced toward Daron. It was ten minutes before lights out, so mostly everybody was in bed. Daron came forward.

"That's what I thought. All you niggas do is talk." Santana went and sat down in his chair, awaiting an altercation. All Daron wanted to do was provoke Santana. Daron loved the reaction he got from Santana.

"Fuck you, you lor bitch. They should have killed you and your momma by now. Shorty, your days are numbered!" Daron replied as he kicked off his shoes and laid in his bed.

"You think I'm a bitch or something?" Santana said.

"You got that right, shorty." Daron laughed. Santana grew an-grier by the minute. *I got something for this nigga. Wait until the lights go out.* He continued to prep himself. He slowly tried to gain composure of his temper, but he couldn't. The lights went out, he moved.

Santana ran across the dorm and swung a flurry of hits, landing most of them. Daron was caught defenseless under his covers. All he could do was ball up and wait for help from the staff. Santana got tired of swinging, so he began to talk cash shit.

"Who's the bitch now? You the one calling for help and shit! Fuck you, you bitch ass nigga."

Daron didn't speak. He stayed curled up under the covers. Santana heard footsteps toward him. He knew it was the staff, so he didn't need to get aggressive. Backbone was a hand off program.

"Vasquez, grab some things. You're going to the dining hall for the night to cool off." Santana looked at the staff member with a smug grin.

"Whatever." He looked back at Daron still curled up. "Nigga, you a bitch." Daron said nothing. Santana grabbed a pillow, two blankets, some change for the vending machines, and his favorite book—*True to the Game*—written by Terri Woods. As Santana walked by Daron's bed to leave, a large object was swung at him, causing Santana to duck. The staff didn't see the object, so the first thing that came to his mind was that Santana was trying to attack yet again. The staff member tackled Santana to the ground.

"Calm down, Mr. Vasquez. Please calm down!" the staff member begged.

"Get the fuck off of me. I didn't do shit, yo," Santana replied under the guard. Santana heard footsteps approaching hard and fast. He was light weight shook because of the defenseless position he was in. All he heard was: "Get off my nigga." Before the weight rose off of him, Rolando was smashing the officer that just had Santana held down, but the staff member was much too big for Rolando to handle; before long, Rolando found himself crashing against the wall from the heavy shove the staff member had given him. Santana rose to his feet to rock with Daron again but was swiftly restrained by the staff member. This time around, the staff member put Santana in a chokehold that sent him to sleep. Before Rolando could intervene again, other staff members rushed in and subdued Rolando, tasing him to sleep.

Moments later, Santana woke up in cuffs sitting next to Rolando's sprawled out body. Rolando stirred, managing to get up.

"Damn lor yo, you alright?" Rolando asked. He too was in cuffs. Two huge staff members were standing next to them.

"Yeah, I'm good. How about you?" Santana replied as he checked Rolando over.

"Bra, I'm good. You know they 'bout to ship niggas out, right? I just got here, so I can care less, but you only had a month and a half left before you could leave. You're too wild for real, you gotta relax, if you want to go home to ya family!" Rolando said right next to Santana.

"You ain't have to jump in the way you did earlier. The staff really didn't want no problems. That nigga was confused than anything. Plus, he was just trying to calm me down. When I heard your footsteps, I thought you was that hoe ass nigga Daron. That nigga still crumbled me, but its straight. I did me," Santana said with pride.

"We're gonna uncuff you both now, and if you make any funny move, rest assured you'd regret it," one of the huge staff members said.

"Is that clear?" the other staff member said, eyeing them.

"Clear," Rolando and Santana chorused.

The staff members uncuffed them and trained their eyes on the two boys while retreating from the room, leaving the two to themselves.

Rolando began: "I fuck with you, shorty, and if some bullshit look like it's about to pop, I'm there. I was there like any real nigga should have been. I don't fuck with a lot of niggas, blood, but I fuck with you. You're a loyal—" Rolando's words were cut short as two men walked up. One of the men was of slim build while the other one was stocky.

"Mr. Vasquez?" the stocky one said.

"What's up?" Santana answered.

"I'm Mr. McDonald, and this is Mr. Blankson—my P.A. I'm the director of this camp and to my knowledge you tried to start a riot last night in my dorms. Before then I hear you was a good student, a little of a temper, but very respectful. Unfortunately, you'll be transferred back to The Charles H. Hickey School for boys waiting further placement. I ask that you cooperate with my officers on the way back. Again, Mr. Vasquez, sorry it turned out like this, but I must retain order. Good luck." Mr. McDonald left the office. Santana sighed. *At least Rolando didn't get kicked out because of me.* It was the only affirmation he could give himself for his dumb ass actions.

"You be safe down there, shorty. Tijuana gone be mad, but she loves you so you should be straight," Rolando said. All Santana could do was prepare mentally for the bullshit he was about to endure. The staff member that stood guard grabbed Santana's arm, indicating his time to leave. Santana nodded at Rolando, a soldier's goodbye.

"Be safe, lor bro, and get home to ya moms." Santana took Rolando's words of advice as he was led out of the building to the waiting van. Physically drained, Santana hopped in the van. As soon as he got comfortable, he laid his head against the barred window and drifted off to sleep, for once in a peaceful mind state.

Santana sat in the bull pen awaiting housing. Ms. Thomas already let Santana know what was on her mind only minutes earlier. She had called Tijuana after she cursed him out for being back, so Mandella Hall was probably his next destination. Santana knew what he was in for, a barrage of chastisement, maybe even an ass whipping. He knew Tijuana was on her way to pick him up and talk shit. As the thoughts ran through his head, Tijuana walked through the door to the bull pen. He wasn't ready for the Tijuana that walked through the gate of the bull pen. The disappointed look on her face killed him. *I can only imagine what my mom's gone look like.* He looked at her; she looked back. He needed her to say something.

"What, ma? Say something. That silent treatment shit not working." He tried to play tough. Still, she said nothing and opened the gate. He stood and walked through the gate awaiting his next order. He was happy to see Tijuana, but she was acting brand new. He knew he fucked up but there was no need to be scolded for something he couldn't change. He would speak his mind once they were alone and out of ear shot. Right now, she had the torch. They moved through the hall toward *Control*. Once they were out of camera view, Tijuana unleashed a flurry of smacks to his head.

"Oh shit." He laughed at her anger. She stopped instantly.

"This shit ain't funny, Santana. I'm not playing with you. You was going home with ya bad ass. You were so close." Tijuana was annoyed. Truth be told, Santana enjoyed the attention. Tijuana was his baby; she just worried too much. They continued the walk to *Control*. She shackled his ankles and boarded the van. Tijuana had a lot she wanted to talk about. One being about a dude named Andre Jones. She tried to explain a little on the way to Mandella. Andre Jones was arrested in Philly for her brother's murder. Blaze was in another jail in protected custody. Dre was extradited to Hickey but moved the same night because of the relationship between Tijuana and Kane. That confused Santana, but he let it pass. Tijuana saw the look on his face, so she explained.

"I see that look on your face about Dre not being allowed here. Well, the admin people feel like I put a hit out on Blaze, but they can't prove it. So, to take "extra precaution" like they say, they moved him to Cheltenham—a juvenile jail in Prince George's County in Maryland." He could tell Tijuana was getting agitated. Santana sat and adsorbed everything she was saying.

"What about Drew?" Santana asked.

"They dropped the charges of attempted murder and sent him to Glen Mills for their twelve-month program. His crazy ass probably won't last either. You two lor niggas need guidance." Tijuana laughed, for the first time in a long time. He could tell even though she was still mad at him for being kicked out of the camps, she was happy to have him back.

The van pulled up in front of Mandella Hall. Santana stepped out after his shackles were taken off his ankles. The air in Baltimore was different than the air in Garrett County, Maryland. In an odd way Santana felt like he was back home, where he needed to be. He stretched and looked around. *Yeah, it's back at square one*, he told himself as he and Tijuana walked the small distance to the entrance. The atmosphere was the same as when he left the first time. There were new faces, but some of the same people. Geezy approached Santana, welcoming him back.

"Crazy to see you, but welcome back to the hood, lor yo." What caught Santana for a loop was Bumpy. Last time the two talked, he and Drew was stomping him out. The nigga walked by and nodded as if to say, "What's up?" *These niggas got me fuck up. They think because my nigga gone, I won't ride on' 'em. Yeah, a'ight.* Tijuana recognized the look all too well by now. Santana was ready to fight. Tijuana grabbed Santana by the arm.

"Get your lor crazy ass over here so you can call Simfany." *Damn, they on a first name basis now. I'm fucked.* He laughed. That calmed him down a lot. He really didn't care, but he knew that everything he did would be reported back to his mother. Tijuana dialed Simfany's number by memory. She handed Santana the receiver when the other party picked up the call.

"Hello?" Simfany answered.

"Yeah," Santana answered, expecting Simfany to go off on him.

"Who the fuck is this?" she asked

"Santana," he replied.

"Oh, boy, you almost got hung up on. What's up?" she asked. Santana looked up at Tijuana. She hadn't told Simfany he was kicked out the camps; she left that on him.

"I'm good, but they kicked me out of the Backbone last night. Before you start going crazy, it was my fault. I fucked up. Excuse my language. I let this nigga get under my skin, so I fought him. Shit got out of hand though. It seems like everybody took that opportunity to fight, getting me booted. Sorry I fucked up." Simfany sighed.

"When will you learn to stop fighting and come home? Huh. Momma miss you, Tana. When did you become so violent anyway? You're starting to act too much like your father. Anyway, I'm not mad—just disappointed. I just want you here with me. Regardless of the fact that you continue to fuck up, I still love you, Santana. Please stay out of trouble." "Damn, you rushing me off the phone now?" Santana was vexed.

"Nigga, I dare you to act like you got an attitude. I'm on the turn pike right now on my way to the city. I need to get off the phone. The state troopers out tonight. I don't have time to be pulled over. Call me sometime tomorrow. I'll be around Justice and Lonnie. You need to talk to that little boy, something going on with him. Look, I gotta go. Tell Tijuana I send my love and for her to take care of my baby. Love you."

"A'ight, love you too." Santana put the phone back in its cradle. *Bet I won't pass off that message,* he told himself.

"My mom sends her love," was all Santana relayed. Santana had a lot of thinking to do, so he went to his cell and thought about everything in a nutshell. He just thought about life in general. This new man he had become was a shield from danger, but he adapted to the mentality, making it his own. He did more than adapt; he became the aggressor. How he saw it was: kill or be killed, ride or get rolled over. He hated that, but he picked survival overall.

Santana's thoughts were interrupted by Bumpy and a couple of his friends. Santana looked up at the door frame where Bumpy stood.

"What's good, my G?" Santana rose to his feet. He pressed his back against the wall, awaiting an attack.

"Shit, blood, you tell me. You were riding with that blue flame nigga hard. Now you solo, you ain't got shit to say. I find that funny!" Bumpy said venomously.

"Nah, nigga, that's what you assume. My niggas don't make me. I am who I am. I back down from no nigga. I ain't really got too much more rap, if you ask me." Santana stood his ground. It was four on one, but the odds didn't matter. It was what it was. It wouldn't be the first time he was jumped.

"Say no more." Bumpy advanced. Santana wasted no time and rushed him, picking Bumpy off his feet. Santana and Bumpy fell into the hall. Santana tucked his head into Bumpy's chest to take pressure off the blows he knew was coming. The other three tried to pull Santana off of Bumpy, but Santana had a death grip hold of him. They began to beat the side of Santana head and body. Santana couldn't take too much more; he bit down into Bumpy's chest.

Bumpy let out a loud scream, causing his posse to raise up. In that split moment, Santana started punching Bumpy as hard as he could in the face. His attack gave Bumpy's men complete access to his own face. Santana took some blows then went back to his original position. *Fuck!* was all he could think as he felt blow after blow land on the side of his head.

"Y'all niggas in here trippin' for real," Santana heard in the distance. The blows began to slowly stop with their fatigue.

"Bumpy, you know Rolando would have torn your ass up if he would have seen you on his lor nigga." The voice sounded familiar, but Santana couldn't place it. Regardless, Santana's head stayed balled into Bumpy's chest.

"Get this lor nigga off of me," Bumpy pleaded. Santana felt a set of hands grabbing at him; nonetheless, he didn't budge.

"Lor yo, let go, I got you." Santana looked up and saw Glen, his old cell mate. He had no choice but to trust his word. Glen grabbed Santana and pushed him into his room. Bumpy got up with his nose bloody, chest bleeding and an eye almost swollen shut." Bumpy was furious.

"It is what it is, Bumpy. What's the funny part? You was a swine when my niggas was here. Now all of a sudden you're a super blood. Nigga, suck my dick!" Santana spat at him. Geezy stayed in front of the door, trying to keep Santana in his room.

"Look, shorty, you niggas trippin. Kev, get this nigga. This shit was over months ago. The lor nigga didn't back down, let 'em live!" Geezy said.

"Fuck them niggas. You ain't got to plead shit for me!" Santana barked. Bumpy walked away without speaking another word. His goons followed. Geezy waited until they all was gone before he spoke. Santana was seated on the floor running his fingers through his hair.

"You a'ight, lor yo?" Geezy asked.

"Nigga, I'm good. You a'ight?" Santana asked with venom in his voice. Once again, he felt like it was him against all. And Geezy caught on.

"Lor yo, I'm on ya side, shorty. I ain't beefing with you. Imma let you calm down because you trippin. Holla at me tomorrow. Stay on point though. Just remember I'm not against you," Geezy explained as he was leaving the room. Santana stayed on guard all night until he was too restless, and he had to succumb to sleep.

Jamel Mitchell

Chapter Five

Simfany arrived in New York around 10:00 p.m. Everything still looked the same as it did before she left. *The city that never sleeps; it felt good to be back in familiar territory,* she thought as she drove down Park Avenue looking for a place to park. She quickly thought better of it and took Courtland Avenue to Clay Avenue. Simfany didn't want anybody to know what she was driving. She parked her car on Clay Avenue and caught a cab to Melrose. Before she departed from her car, she made sure she was well equipped with a cream-colored vest and two Glock 26's. *Safety is before all,* she reminded herself as she grabbed the hardware. Byrd had taught her well. She would rather be overprotective than be unprotected. As the cab pulled up to the side of building 304, Simfany took close awareness of her surroundings. Word was that the two hoods that both claimed Courtland became one. Jackson and Melrose was right across the street from each other. The only thing that separated them was Morris Avenue. Since Emilio's death there was nobody that tried to take the Avenue over. Simfany didn't know how true it was but at the end of the day she really didn't care. She paid her fare and exited the cab. She walked to her old building and rung the bell for Lonnie's apartment.

"Who is it?" a strong Spanish-accented woman called out through the monitor.

"It's Simfany, baby girl," Simfany replied into the box.

"Simfany who?"

"*Simfany,* bitch, open the damn door." She laughed as the door buzzed, letting Simfany and another man inside the building. The only thing she didn't miss was the smell of the projects.

Everywhere you went it smelled like piss. As she walked to the elevator, the same elevator she grew up taking, she knew she had been gone for too long. She wanted the city life back. It was a rush that she got for being back, she couldn't even explain it if she wanted to. As Simfany waited on the elevator, she checked the clips in the Glock 26's. *Fully loaded.* The elevator finally came, taking Simfany to the eighth floor, the floor Lonnie lived on. Simfany walked out of the elevator with both her hands occupied with steel in them. Ever since she had got shot, she stayed extra cautious of her surroundings. It was starting to reach the point of being dangerous of her and others. She had nobody to tell her that, so she did what needed to be done. Simfany walked the distance to Lonnie's apartment; she knocked on the door. The peep hole got dark, indicating someone was looking out the peep hole. Before she had a chance to react or pull her strap, the door swung open and Justice was all over her. Her paranoia was getting the best of her. She almost upped her strap on Justice's bad ass. She smiled; at least she knew somebody missed her besides Santana. Justice hugged her and didn't let go for a while.

"Little boy, if you don't let me go I'm gone beat that ass," Simfany teased.

"Damn, auntie, you acting all funny now."

"I miss you, son, for real. How my nigga doing? I wanted to come to Baltimore but mom wouldn't let me." Justice ran off at the mouth rapidly. He moved out of the way to let Simfany in.

"Where ya momma?" Simfany asked.

"She went to the store. She been gone a little second she should be back soon," he said in a matter-of-fact kind of tone. Simfany's facial expression twisted.

"So, who was that on the intercom?" Simfany asked curiously.

"Oh, that was my girl. You passed her in the living room. She was sitting on the couch waiting for me to come back. Come on, I'll introduce you to her." They walked back up front to the living room. Simfany looked into the room and saw the pretty girl sitting on the couch playing with her nails.

"So, you couldn't speak?" Simfany said bluntly.

"Simfany!" Justice nudged her. He was getting embarrassed.

"My bad. How are you doing today, beautiful? My name is Simfany and yours?"

"Destiny," the girl on the couch replied.

"Destiny, has this little light-skinned nigga been treating you right?" That made her new friend laugh.

"I mean he treats me alright. I heard a lot about you, well respected out here. That's good being a female from the hood. My fault for not speaking, but your nephew happened to be working my last nerve tonight." Simfany looked back at Justice to let him know about himself but thought twice of it when she saw his devil eyes. The devil eyes meant he was pissed. Simfany laughed and dipped out before the two clashed.

"Nice to meet you again, Destiny, please keep him out of trouble." And with that Simfany went into the back to wait on Lonnie. Simfany could hear the two arguing. She heard the front door open then slam. Simfany walked to the living room to make sure all was well. She found Destiny in the same position as she was only minutes prior, only this time she was crying her eyes out.

"You alright, baby girl?" Simfany asked.

"I'm good, but he can be so mean at times." Destiny sniffled.

"You smoke?" Simfany asked as she pulled out an already rolled joint.

"Yeah." Destiny wiped the tears off her face and smiled as she answered.

"Come on. Hurry up before Lonnie get back." Simfany grabbed her hand and ran to the back room. Simfany tossed Destiny the joint and lighter to spark up. Destiny happily obliged and lit up. As Simfany and Destiny smoked their pain away, niggas was lurking in the hood. What with the eerie atmosphere, a face was bound to end up on *RIP* T-shirt before the night was over. Justice left the apartment angrily because of Destiny's smart-ass mouth. He was vexed. For her to be two years older than him, she acted like a child. Every day it was a new drama between the two. *I had to leave before I snapped on that bitch,* he thought as he ran down the stairs to the lobby. He didn't know where he was going but he knew he had to get out of that house before he said or did something he would later regret.

He knew he needed a second to breathe. Destiny was an extremely beautiful girl, but she came with too much at times. Destiny was all that ran through his mind as he walked through the hood. He saw a dice game popping in the big park, so he made his way over there to get his hands in something. As he approached, he saw a lot of his old friends standing around watching. Valhalla was deep tonight. Justice tried not to pay attention, but it was inevitable, they were everywhere. Big E and Bogus was also in presence. Still, Justice walked through and showed love to everyone but Bogus. They disliked each other so they just looked at one another and said nothing. Justice looked up to Bogus once upon a time ago, but Simfany had warned him to leave the streets alone or be dealt with accordingly. At first, he played by the rules, but had his hands in a few things, nothing major. Nothing he did went unnoticed.

Bogus was known in the hood for putting in work, so Justice kept his ratchet on him at all times. It was just in case a nigga felt like he was God and wanted to snatch his life; he would be prepared. Walking up into a crowd of Valhalla niggas showed a sign of arrogance; the boy had balls. Bogus was upset to see the little nigga out amongst his family, but he kept cool and held his composure. With nothing else to do and money to spare, Justice hopped in the dice game. As time passed by, people began to slowly drift off. Justice got so caught up in the game he didn't realize it was only him and two other people shooting. One of those people happened to be Bogus.

"Put fifty on it, nigga," Justice said as he looked Bogus in the eyes.

"Shoot' em, holla." Bogus dropped his money to the pavement. Justice rolled a seven, his first roll. He collected his money. Without any further conversation Bogus dropped another fifty-dollar bill to the pavement. Justice rolled again. His point this time was a six.

"I got a buck say you miss ya point!" Bogus dropped another big face to the ground.

Justice looked at Bogus. *Fuck it,* he thought putting a hundred-dollar bill on the ground too. The other dude that was still there slid off, seeing that Bogus and Justice was getting personal. Justice rolled a five.

"That's *my* number. Keep shooting." Bogus talked to the dice.

"Nigga, you know what comes next." Justice got amped also. He rolled again. Justice's heart raced; he was nervous. He wasn't letting Bogus leave with his money, so he prayed that he won. Justice rolled again, a four. Justice's heart felt like it wanted to jump out of his chest.

It wasn't just about the money; it was about beating Bogus and making a statement. But if truth be told, it was also about the money. Justice rolled and struck the six he'd been waiting on. Justice reached down and scooped up his money.

"Good hit, son, good hit. Shoot it back." Bogus threw more money on the ground. It was just an amusement for him.

"Shit, I'm good, I'm 'bout to go home. It's too late already. You'll be able to win some of this bread tomorrow. But my nigga, I'm gone. If I lost I was leaving; so, if I win it's no different."

Bogus nodded. "Hit and run, huh? It's cool. Run home before Lonnie come out this bitch looking for you ready to whoop that ass," Bogus teased.

"Damn, you shooting at me like that! Keep playing with me, Bogus." Justice leveled up with him.

"Or what, *Mr. I'm-only-fourteen*! Huh? Nigga, you lucky I let ya young ass live out here." Bogus spit venom at Justice. Justice's devil's eyes became visible.

"Oh, so you mad? Nigga, fuck you!" Bogus taunted again. Justice spit at Bogus, barely missing him. Bogus advanced; Justice upped his gun and pointed at Bogus and trained it at head level. Bogus looked death in its eyes.

"Damn, you pulling guns out on family now? Nigga, I'm the reason your bitch ass still alive. Me! And you pull out ya ratchet on me? My nigga, what happened to your heart and loyalty? The game is played differently by each player. It's all love though. Kill me, Justice, if that's what you want to do. Do your thing, son." Bogus looked hurt. Going against his better judgment, Justice put the gun back into his waist band.

"My bad, Bogy," Justice said and ran off. Justice left the big park and beelined back to his building. As he came around 321, he saw a group of niggas in front of his building and got paranoid. *How the fuck am I gone get out of this shit? And how the hell am I going to get inside this building?* he contemplated. Justice pulled his gun out; he pulled the barrel back to put a shell in the head. The irony of the situation was that Bogus had gave him the gun a year or two ago. Justice knew he was tripping not having a bullet in the chamber. It was the only reason Bogus was still breathing. Justice walked the long way behind 700, trying to get to the back of his building without being seen. Justice hated the back exit to the building, but it was his only way to make it inside. Justice crept past the 700 building; he was in the parking lot of the Melrose Community Center located in the back of his building 304. He waited patiently for any signs of movement.

He looked for shadows; he looked for anything that would harm him. He continued to wait; he saw nothing, so he made his move. Justice hopped the small black fence and made his way down the ramp to the back of the building. What he didn't know was that somebody else waited patiently in the cut for him to fuck up. Justice didn't notice the figure behind him until it was too late. The dark figure raised his gun as he slowly crept closer. Justice felt a presence and looked behind him. Without second thought he took off. A single shot followed. *Bock!* Another shot rang, hitting Justice in his lower back. *Bock!* He collapsed, unable to grab for his gun. The dark figure walked up on him and bent down. Justice turned over to look his killer in his eyes. He searched the eyes for remorse but found none. He wondered who was on the other end of that mask. *Fuck! This shit hurt. I wonder who Bogus sent to send me to my maker.* His thoughts ran wild in the split seconds he had left. His emotions got the best of him. He started to cry, knowing that the life he knew was fading away by degrees. He reached out and grabbed the mask off the face of the reaper's face. The face looking back at him hurt more than the bullets that pierced his flesh.

"Peewee—" was all Justice got to say before he was shot point-blank in his face. Peewee wiped the tears from his eyes as he grabbed his ski mask out of Justice's grip and ran off leaving every memory they shared in blood.

"Simfany, did you hear that shit?" Destiny asked. Instinct made her get up and look out the window. *That shit sounded closer than a muthfucka.* Destiny was high, but she could have sworn she saw somebody running from behind the center. *Oh well,* she told herself. She sat back down waiting on joint number four to slide through. Lonnie had come back home within a few minutes of Justice's departure. When she came in, Destiny and Simfany were in her room blowing smoke in the air. At first Destiny was shook, but quickly got over it when Lonnie sat down and hopped in the cipher. A cold chill ran down Destiny's back. Destiny felt like her soul was being ripped out of her. She had to take a deep breath. She couldn't understand the feeling she was having. The room suddenly turned cold. To make sure she wasn't tripping she had to ask the obvious.

"Is it me or is it cold in here?" Destiny asked. Both Simfany and Lonnie looked at her as if she was losing her marbles.

"You okay, ma?" Simfany asked first.

"Yeah, but I swear it got colder in this bitch. Plus those guns shots felt closer than normal. Plus I know I saw somebody running away from the back of the building. I'm tripping, I hope. I just got an eerie feeling, ma. That's all. I don't mean to blow ya high." Destiny explained. Her paranoia knocked her high out the box; she was on the alert.

"I don't know but if Justice's ass is not in this house in the next hour, I'm gone shoot that nigga myself. Pass that blunt, Chula." Lonnie was high; all she wanted to do is clown.

"Lonnie, I'm worried about Justice. He don't stay out this late ever." Destiny began to get scared not only for her, but for Justice. They say when you really love someone, you feel the same pain each other goes through. She felt that something was wrong; she didn't really know what but she felt *it.* Destiny took a round of deep breaths and eventually calmed herself down. She decided to chill and relax with her mother-in-law and aunt-in-law. They smoked until they all passed out. Still, there was no sign of Justice, but the women were too high to actually notice. Simfany was awakened out of her slumber by Lonnie's hysterical crying.

Instinctively, Simfany grabbed her gun and walked to the kitchen in her bra and panties. As she walked into the kitchen, she heard the blaring sound of a police scanner or walkie talkie; she wasn't sure. Simfany could hear the officer(s) talking to Destiny in the living room. She hurried to the back to get dressed so she could see what was going on. That eerie feeling Destiny had the night before ran through Simfany's thoughts. Simfany walked back up front towards the living room to find Lonnie in the kitchen crying her eyes out.

"Chula, what's going on?" Simfany asked. She got a blank stare. She could tell in her best friend's eyes that Lonnie was lost in her own world.

"Lonnie, are you okay?" she asked yet again.

"Baby girl, what's wrong?" Simfany asked. The look in Lonnie's eyes said it all. Simfany panicked and ran straight to Justice's room. His bed was still made from the day before. *Please, God, let this child be okay,* she prayed. Simfany ran back into the kitchen. She thought about Santana the whole way. Justice's room was only 20 feet from the kitchen, but the run felt like a mile. Lonnie continued to cry; it seemed as if the sobs was getting harder. Simfany didn't know what to say or do. She didn't understand what was going on. In the hood people only cry like this when two things happen. Either their loved one killed someone and they know it's over for them or their loved one is the one that got killed. And whether she wanted to accept it or not, she automatically thought the worst.

"Calm down, baby, you gotta tell me what's going on, Lonnie. Please. You're scaring me."

Simfany begged. Lonnie rocked back and forth, singing gospel music to herself in her native tongue, Spanish.

"Momma, tell me what's going on." Lonnie was stuck in a daze. Simfany bent down and kissed Lonnie on her head as she made her way into the living room to get the information she needed. Her Juicy Couture pants stopped the officer in mid-sentence as she walked in. Everyone in the room looked up as Simfany made her presence known. Destiny was on the couch crying silent tears, as she answered the detective's questions. Destiny looked up, and Simfany's heart broke. She opened her arms and motioned for Destiny to come to her. Destiny wept her way into Simfany's awaiting arms. Simfany knew the answer to her questions before she even asked them.

"What's going on, officer, that has my sister and my nephew's girlfriend so distraught? What kind of trouble has Justice got into now?" Simfany. She got the confirmation of her suspicions when the detectives looked at each other in confusion. Neither detective responded.

"Ahh, excuse me! What the fuck is going on!" she shouted. Simfany's emotions began to catch up with her. She started to cry.

"Please officer tell me what's going on," she begged.

"I'm sorry to tell you this, but Justice Torres was murdered last night behind this very building. We don't—" The detective's words went blank as Simfany's thoughts came crashing down on her. The tears that came out of her eyes came in streams. *My baby! Please, God, don't do this to us. Please, God, I beg you.* She couldn't believe what she heard. But she knew the whole time with everyone crying and looking like death touched their lives. Now death had touched her life again. It seemed like death followed her around and played with everybody's life that was close to her or even around her. She gathered herself together to find out more.

"So, let me get this right, you just looked me in my muthafuckin face and told me my nephew was killed last night. Is that right?" Simfany asked again to make sure she heard the shit right.

"Ma'am, unfortunately, yes, Justice Torres was a victim of a homicide last night." Simfany hugged Destiny tighter to conceal her frustration. She really didn't understand what to do, what to ask, or what information they may need.

"But he was just here!" she cried. "My baby was just here." *Why does this awful shit keep happening around me?* she seriously asked herself. The women held each other until they could gather their thoughts to console Lonnie. Lonnie, Santana, Peewee and Destiny was all she could grip her mind around, the five people that would feel his death the most and take it the hardest. *Santana can't catch a break. Lonnie lost her only son and Peewee lost two best friends, one to the jail system and the other to an early grave.* Simfany cried harder when she thought about Peewee.

He was a lost soul that needed help. Of the two people that really loved that boy, one was locked up and the other ended up dead.

Simfany was devastated. This murder was going to destroy five other lives. Simfany tried to get a grip of herself and sat down on the closest thing to her. She was hurting, but she needed every detail that they could provide.

"Please tell me everything you know so far," Simfany demanded.

"Ma'am, no disrespect intended, but are you of blood relation to the deceased?" the officer asked.

"What the fuck did I say when I first came into this muthafuckin living room? He is my fucking nephew!" Simfany shouted.

"Ma'am, you don't have to yell, I apologize to you. I understand that losing a love on especially so young is hard, but—"

Simfany looked to the other officer present and asked:

"Can you please let me know what you have so far regarding my *nephew's* murder?"

The officer Simfany was talking to extended his hand as a greeting and a white flag.

"My name is Detective Hill. I work for the Bronx Homicide Division." Simfany hesitantly extended her hand.

"Simfany Vasquez." Simfany waited for the officer to continue.

"Oh, excuse me. So far what we have is an eyewitness saying that Justice was in a confrontation last night with Bernard "Bogus" Tru. The witness says that Mr. Torres pulled out a gun on Tru over a dice game. But here is where we are lost at, ten minutes later shots were fired and Torres was murdered. Bernard was in the store on 153rd and Courtland Avenue at the time of the actual shooting, excluding him as a suspect. It's all too confusing right now. We have Mr. Tru downtown right now answering questions as we speak. That's where I'm at in my investigation. When there is an update, we will let Ms. Torres know and she can later tell you. I beg that you let us handle this investigation, Ms. Vasquez, and not take the law into your own hands. No matter how long it takes, we will catch this person that killed your nephew. The streets always talk and we listen. You ladies hold it together. We will be trying our best. And please give this card to Ms. Torres and tell her to call if she thinks of anything else. Thank you." Simfany remained calm as Destiny let the two officers out. *Is it me or was that last comment about the law directed at me?* Simfany thought about her own past. The slamming of the door brought Simfany out of her daze.

Lonnie. Simfany got up and prepared herself mentally to talk to Lonnie. Simfany walked into the kitchen thinking Lonnie was still there, but she had only saw a crying Destiny looking out of the kitchen window at the beautiful brisk day. She was really tripping now. *How the fuck did she get past me without me—You know what? Fuck it.* She debated with herself. She walked to the back, to Lonnie's room. The room was empty. The bathroom door was open so there was no need to check there. Simfany went to the other only place she could be unless she left the house. *Justice's room.* As Simfany walked into the room, she saw Lonnie curled up on Justice's bed holding his elementary school graduation picture of him, Peewee and Santana. It crushed her to see her best friend so devastated. She could understand because if the roles were reversed, she would be tripping also. Simfany grabbed a blanket out the closet in the hall and placed it over Lonnie's body. Simfany sighed as she bent down and kissed her friend on the forehead. She walked to the door but stopped briefly and turned around. She thought she heard something; it was Lonnie mumbling in her sleep. Simfany couldn't make out what she was saying, so she moved closer. Lonnie's mumbling continued until she audibly said: "Mommy loves you, baby." Simfany cried silent tears as she quietly left the room, leaving Lonnie at peace.

Jamel Mitchell

Chapter Six

Santana awoke, sitting bolt upright, gasping for breath, heart racing. For a quick second it felt like his body had shutdown. He wiped the sweat from his forehead and tried to calm his mind. He couldn't explain the feeling, but it felt as if someone was holding him to his bed.

After he calmed down, he chucked it up to being the product of a bad dream. All was okay. Santana got out of his bed and went to the big bathroom to handle his morning duties. Santana sat at the end of his bed as he combed his hair and rapped to himself. Caught up in the lyrics of the song, he didn't see Tijuana in the doorway. She just stared at the growing boy in front of her. The child she first met was different than the child she held her gaze on. They were night and day. While Santana had a lot of charisma when he first arrived, he was starting to mature and build confidence while developing into his new role as a young man. His shield, as he called it, made him into a little warrior. She smiled, wishing there were many more like him. Tijuana knocked on the door frame to get his attention. Santana jumped; he was startled.

"Do you ever get any time for yourself?" he thought out loud. Tijuana laughed. She understood how true that was.

"Fuck ya nappy headed ass. And yeah, I go home, but not as much. I don't have anything waiting for me there." Neither dabbled into that conversation.

"Today's my overtime day anyway," she said with a cute smile on her face.

"Damn, ma, you just went crazy on the kid." They both broke the ice and shared a laugh.

Tijuana's face got sullen as if she was troubled about something. Santana knew her all too well; it was a sign that she wanted to talk about something serious.

"What's on ya mind, ma?" Santana asked. "What's bothering you?"

"Dre and Blaze go to get indicted today. I don't know if I want to go see what's going on or not. They say Blaze is supposed to testify at the indictment hearing." Santana didn't understand the importance of the event, so he kept his comments to himself. Regardless, he would show support. He knew what the process was. He just couldn't understand why Tijuana was so out of it.

"It's only a court hearing, right?"

"Yeah, but once Blaze gets under oath at the indictment hearing, and they informally indict Dre on a murder charge, they will let Blaze possibly go free. I'm not afraid of the nigga, but he is the reason my brother got killed. So I feel some type of way of course."

"I can understand. You know he not gone step foot in that county, so you'll be straight," Santana said assuringly.

"I hope so," Tijuana replied, still leaning in his doorway.

"Oh, and before I go, I heard about last night too. When will you stop?" Tijuana asked.

"Fuck is you talking about?" Santana acted as if he didn't know what she was talking about.

"Fighting, nigga. Stop fucking fighting!"

"You worried about all the wrong shit right now, ma. We can talk about my issues some other time. Agreed? Today about you, so relax and think positive."

"I can feel that, but nigga, ya lor ass ain't slick."

"I'll be up to eat in a second," Santana said, dismissing Tijuana.

"Bye to you too then." She laughed, then strutted away. Hearing that Blaze would be out put an ounce of fear in Santana's heart. The afterthought of riding on Blaze didn't seem too harmful until now. Since his mother had told him about the possible connection between her and the T.T.P. niggas, he also dreaded this day. They say your soul feels when something bad is about to happen. Maybe that dream he just had concerned his mother. He stopped short and thought.

For the first time in a long time, Santana got on his feet and prayed. He prayed to his God for his protection, mercy and guidance.

***

Dre sat at the defense table calculating what his life would be like if he had not pulled that trigger. It crushed him to the core to know his nigga was willing to bury him. *Karma is a muthafucka,* he thought. Today, regardless of how he felt, he had no say in the matter. He was solely there on the fact to be indicted and make a plea. Dre hoped Blaze saved face and refused to testify at the hearing. The grand jury wouldn't see his statement, and other than his statement they had nothing. Nobody else was there, so nobody else came forward. Ty was the only other witness. The last eyewitness was the nigga he loved like a brother but feared all in the same breath.

Dre waited patiently as the hearing began. He listened to the white folks give their version of a monster that killed a man in cold blood. They went on and on indicating about the gang violence that had plagued the youth in Harford County. They made Dre sound menacing. It was nothing he could do but listen. He only agreed to be there to see if Blaze was going to do his thing. He heard the rumors but he had to witness the shit with his own two eyes.

The time had come for Blaze to give his account of the events of that night. Dre heard Blaze's name being called for by bailiff. It took only a couple of seconds for Blaze to walk in handcuffed and shackled. They sat him in the sector of the court room near the grand jury. He was one of them at the moment, so he had to be protected. Until Blaze was called upon to take the stand, Dre watched his every move and emotion. Blaze kept his head down. He refused to make eye contact.

Dre just watched as Blaze went under oath and the questions began. Why did Mr. Jones pull the trigger? What provoked him to kill Kane Moore? Was this a gang issue? The questions came rapidly and Blaze answered each of them truthfully as possible. He left out nothing.

"Do you see the person who murdered Kane Moore in this court room today, and if so please point him out and describe what he has on." A tear fell from Dre's eye as Blaze pointed at him, describing his jail house wardrobe. He looked at Blaze; Blaze looked back as his finger stayed raised stuck in the air. *I killed to save your life, so you decide to take mine? Real nigga shit,* he thought. They no longer needed Blaze to be a stool pigeon. The work was done. Blaze got off the stand and began to exit the court room. He looked up and mouthed *Sorry* to Dre. That took Dre over the loop; he went crazy.

"You bitch ass nigga, you sorry? Nigga, I killed for you! Not me, but for you, shorty. You a ratting ass bitch, shorty. Die slow, pussy. Don't ever get locked up again because I promise if you come anywhere, I'm at you and you will join Kane." He sat back down. His lawyer was frantic. His lawyer's opinion didn't really matter no more. How he saw it with Blaze's testimony—it was a no-win situation. His life was over. He threw his life away for a nigga he loved but didn't have the same love for him. Blaze kept walking. He could care less about Dre's ranting and raving; he knew his freedom was only hours away.

Dre pleaded not guilty despite Blaze's testimony. The court then moved for Dre to be waived up so he could stand trial as an adult. He knew it was coming eventually, so he wasn't surprised.

By the time Dre was booked in the Harford County Detention Center, Blaze was leaving the Carter Center in Easton Shore, MD. *At last, I'm a free man*, he thought. After Dre was processed, he was given a free phone call. He called Diana and had her three-way Hood Ru. He waited patiently for Hood to pick up.

"Who this?" Hood asked tiredly.

"Dre on the phone for you," Diana cut in before Dre had the chance to. He knew she would listen to this whole conversation, so he didn't even bother to ask her to put the receiver down.

"What's good, bull?"

"Shit, to be honest—stressed, cuz."

"Did that nut ass nigga take the stand?" Even though the statement was out, he hoped Blaze tried to save some face. He didn't want to have Blaze's blood on his hands.

"Yeah, that nigga a cold-hearted rat, shorty. He told all, but it's all love though. Everything happened for a reason. Niggas of his caliber get to live right, right?" Dre asked in some kind of code.

"I got you, bull, the love you showed won't go unnoticed, even if that nigga turned on you. I got you. Rest easy, my nigga. Me and mine gone make sure you and ya wife straight," Hood promised.

"Good looking, shorty. You stay one hundred, I'm gone," Dre replied.

"You too, bull, you too." Hood hung up.

"Make sure the money they give you; you buy a better lawyer than this piece of shit they trying to give me. I'm trying to give these people a fight. It's his word against mine." Dre stressed every bit of those words to Diana. Though he sounded hopeful, he knew full well that he had no chance."

"You just stay out of trouble in there so I can come see you, and I'll handle my end. I'm not going anywhere so please don't stress over all the wrong shit. I need you sharp and on point. I love you." Diana started to cry.

"Shorty, you know how that makes me feel when you start crying. Please—I'm good. You keep *that thing* tight and we have no issue, you got me?" he asked playfully, trying to lighten up her mood.

"I got you, daddy." She sniffled. He could hear the smile approach her face. "Please be safe, Dre."

"No worries, shorty, I will." The phone went dead. Their time was up, not only his phone time but also Blaze's time. That was only if he hadn't left Maryland already. Only time would tell. Dre sat back and waited for the shit to play itself out.

***

Shortly after lunch, Santana posted up in the multipurpose room waiting next on the Xbox. Geezy and another inmate named Slason were occupied in the new NFL Madden. Santana laughed at the shit they talked to each other. It reminded him of him and Drew. Drew would beat Santana every game, then talk shit. The sad part was that Santana could never beat him, no matter how hard he tried. This was the only pastime on Mandella Hall, besides reading which Santana loved to do. He played basketball, but not often. The passion for the game wasn't the same. He recalled once upon a time basketball being one of his true loves. He still had love for the sport but playing wasn't much fun.

A million and one things ran through Santana's head. When he was worried about his mother, thinking was his coping mechanism. Sometimes it worked; often it didn't. Today was one of the days his thoughts helped. Santana was still worried, but he showed no signs of it. Hours went by; Santana was running the controller by now. He and Slason were in overtime and he had the ball. It came down to the last possession. Santana threw an interception with 45 seconds left in the game. Slason strategically marched the ball down the field, kicking a field goal to win the game. Santana was in his feelings over the pick he threw, but he had to give respect when respect was due.

"Good game, my G. I got last," Santana said, getting back in line to play again. He dapped Slason up before he walked off to take a seat in the back. Before he took his seat he caught out the corner of his eye, Tijuana coming towards him with a look of dismay. The sad look she maintained since her brother passed was heartbreaking, to say the least. Regardless, he continued to be there for her. Tijuana tapped him on the shoulder. He ignored her. She smacked him upside his head. That got him to turn around.

"Damn, ma, you violent." Tijuana smiled. Santana had accomplished his goal.

"What's really good?" he asked, taking his eyes off the game TV.

"Come holla at me for a second. Simfany's trying to talk to you," she replied. Santana's heart dropped. The look on his face told enough of his story.

"She's okay, Tana. Something's wrong with one of your friends. She didn't tell me much. She didn't sound too hurt or frantic." She lied.

"Give me a second. I'll be there."

Tijuana walked back to her office. Santana sat for a couple more plays, then he got up and went to Tijuana's office. He knocked before he entered her office.

"Come in and close the door," she whispered as she talked on the phone. Santana waited. When Tijuana was done talking to Simfany, she passed the phone to him.

"What's up, pretty lady?" Santana asked into the phone.

"Hey, man, how you doing?" Simfany replied with a question of her own.

"I'm good, trying to stay out of trouble. I got into it last night, but I'm a hundred." He laughed, hoping she wouldn't worry.

"Tana, I got bad news." Simfany broke down. Santana looked up at Tijuana for answers. Tijuana had tears in her eyes also.

"Calm down, ma. Talk to me. What are you talking about?" he asked calmly.

"Justice—baby, they killed Justice." Simfany continued to cry. Santana couldn't believe what she said, so he asked her to repeat herself. She did. His heart broke into a million pieces. He cried softly as he listened to his mother. He was sick. His best friend was gunned down at fourteen years old. *Nobody deserves to die at fourteen,* he thought to himself.

"Who killed him, ma?" he asked.

"Nobody knows. The police think Bogus killed him or had him killed. Somebody told the police that Justice pulled a gun out on him over a dice game. I don't know what's going around in the hood."

"Nah, Bogus wouldn't have Justice killed. I don't care what happen. That nigga loved Justice more than he did his own brother. I don't see it happening." Santana sniffled, giving his only tell-tale sign of crying. He worked hard to contain himself. His friend was dead.

"How Peewee taking this shit?" Santana asked.

"Nobody can find him. His mother so gone off drugs she don't know when he coming or going," Simfany answered.

"I'm pretty sure he gone be fucked up over this. If you do see him, call up here so I can talk to him. I need to find out what happened or what the streets is saying happened. Peewee is going kill somebody when the names that are involved start popping out. This shit crazy."

"But the nigga missing in action," Simfany explained again.

"How is Lonnie holding up? And who you have at the house?" Santana asked curiously.

"It's me, Lonnie and Justice's girlfriend. The whole hood fucked up right now. Edwin's holding a vigil for him tonight in the Big Park. After all this is over I 'm coming home. I can't take it. This is starting to become too much for me. You just stay out of trouble and keep your head up okay?"

"I'm good, ma, I promise. I'll talk to you later. I got to get my mind right." Santana's eyes watered. He caught the tear before it got the chance to roll down his face. He handed the phone back to Tijuana, got up then left the office without saying another word. He was crushed. He needed to be alone. He went to his room and locked in.

Once inside his room, he put his face into the pillow and cried for his friends lost soul. He cried until he couldn't produce any more water from his eyes. The death of his best friend hardened his heart. Santana fell asleep reminiscing about everything they'd been through. He also made a promise to himself to kill any and everybody that played a part in Justice's death.

The months flew by, another calendar gone. Body after body was found. Each year that passed made the streets more vicious. Justice's murder overwhelmed Peewee's conscience that he turned the same gun he used to kill Justice on himself. The investigation regarding Justice Torres was closed due to the evidence they found at Peewee's house. Lonnie turned to drugs soon after Peewee committed suicide. She couldn't harbor the stress on her own. With Simfany in a different state and Destiny moving on, the only friend that she had was that *Brown*. The heroin eventually killed Lonnie's mind and self-worth. She walked around Melrose a zombie. The once beautiful Dominican was dead to all. Simfany came back and forth; time after time she tried to render help, but to no avail. The monkey on Lonnie's back overpowered the love they once shared.

Blaze ran from Harford County with no hope of turning back, especially not to testify in Dre's trial. His mother still lived in the "Commons", and that proved to be death in its own right. Hood Ru had so much love for Ms. Harris no one bothered her. But she was warned that if Blaze showed his face anywhere in the county he would die. She understood the code of the streets.

There was only one rule that had to be followed: *No Snitching*! Everything else was fair game. Blaze came back to the county often, slipping in and slipping out. It was never too long, but long enough to be seen by the shadows that lurked within the dark.

Santana finally turned fifteen years old, two years in counting, and he was still fighting and carrying on. Drew got out and came back. Rolando made it home from Back Bone Mountain School only to catch an attempted robbery charge. Santana and Drew eventually became roommates on King Hall (Unit 8), an enhancement unit for youth with more than a year. The life that Santana wanted so badly to be a part of was just beginning.

Carlos continued to hold reign over Baltimore and surprised everyone when he picked Jimdog up on his team. Jimdog filled the spot Byrd once had. Although Byrd was dead and gone, Jimdog was still living in the shadow of his brother. Carlos didn't know for sure if Jimdog killed his brother or not. But Carlos was always taught to keep friends at a distance and your enemies close. Carlos knew he wouldn't be a threat to his organization, so he used him. Carlos wanted Jimdog around as a pawn. If Carlos was right about Jimdog's betrayal, Jimdog's life span was getting shorter and shorter by the passing of each day.

Jamel Mitchell

Chapter Seven

Winter 2004

Blaze drove through Edgewood on his way to his mother's house in Harford Commons. Even though there was a bounty on his head, he came back. From his understanding, his old family (TTP) loved his mother, so he assumed that as long as his mother was around, they wouldn't shoot. Time had passed since his arrest; Dre took a plea for ten years in the state. It was a bargain. Blaze heard through the grape vine that the prosecutor wanted to give Dre forty years, but without Blaze's testimony they had no case. *In Maryland, they make you do 85% of your time, so he would do most of the ten. He was looking at 8 years six months. Not too bad!* Blaze thought as he pulled out his phone and called his mother to indicate that he was near. As Blaze drove past Beacon Terrace, he was spotted by a member of TTP. Not knowing, he continued his ride to his mother's home. Wanda called Hood right away.

"Baby, I just spotted that nigga Blaze riding through the hood. He's probably on his way to see Ms. Harris. Are you close by?" Wanda asked.

"Hold on. I'm looking out the window now. What kind of whip that nigga driving?" Hood asked.

"A black Monte." She tried to yell her response over the blowing wind.

"I think I see that nigga. You sure that's him?" Hood wanted to make sure. The last time he was so-called spotted, he almost killed the wrong nigga.

"Yeah, it's him, babe. Just be careful," Wanda answered.

"I'm good, but if that's bull, I'm gone off that nigga tonight. I'm tired of chasing his nut ass. Good looking, ma. I'll call you later." Hood hung the phone up and went back to the window to make sure Wanda wasn't tripping. He watched as Blaze got out the car and walked into his mother's house. *This nigga got to be crazy,* he told himself. Hood sat down and called Stacks.

"Get everybody to my granny's. Blaze back in town." Hood left no room for questions; he hung the phone up and waited for his family to arrive. Hood looked around the room; it was full of young hitters. He searched the faces of the young members to see any tell-tale sign of fear or betrayal. Blaze tricked them, so why couldn't any of these niggas do the same. He searched their faces a minute or so longer and saw no signs of weakness, then he started his meeting.

"Look, Blaze has been on the menu for quite a while now, once our brother, turned rat. Young bull came back to town with his nut ass. He won't leave alive. I'm gone pick three of you to go with me to end his career. If you're not down with that let me know so you can leave now."

Hood looked around the room, daring someone to raise their hand. He continued.

"You know what you signed up for. I don't send my niggas on missions I won't do myself. I'm still front line. That's why I'm going to prove a point to all the disloyal niggas that's breathing. All I ask is that everybody stay on point especially when *one time* come and start snatching niggas up. And I swear to anybody that let they tongue fly will receive the same fate. Family and all, test me. On a more serious note, let's get this shit done and over with. Love y'all niggas. West Side!" Hood rubbed his hands together as he sat and thought about what needed to be done. *Tonight, it will get done,* he told himself.

Blaze sat at the kitchen table with his mother enjoying the meal she cooked for him. Ms. Harris was concerned for Blaze.

"Narvel, why do you keep bringing your ass back around here? Them boys really want to end your life," Cynthia said, concerned.

"Fuck them niggas. When it's my time to go, I can't stop it. But only God knows."

"All you had to do was remain silent, Narvel. There was nobody else around to tell. Why did you put that kind of hold on your life?" She started to cry. She knew her baby's days were numbered. Blaze grabbed his mother and hugged her.

"What am I supposed to do if you get killed? I can't fight these kids. All I can do is tell the police all that I may know. It may or may not help, but eventually get me killed also. So, tell me what the fuck am I supposed to do if that happens, Narvel!" She shrugged out of his embrace and stood up.

"Until I move you can't come back here, Narvel. You made your bed. You need to be a man and lay in it." Cynthia walked off leaving Blaze lost for words.

"You want me gone! Say no more." Blaze grabbed his car keys and coat. He walked to the front door and looked back at the woman he loved the most in life, his mother. It broke his heart to hear her say the shit she said, but he knew she was right. He unlocked the door to leave. Cynthia walked over to him. She needed to hug her son before he left because she wasn't sure when she would see him again.

"I love you, Narvel," she whispered into his ear as they embraced.

"I love you too, ma." They looked each other over.

"No matter what, you know you're mommy's baby. Just let me come to you from now on, cool?"

"Cool. I love you, ma." Blaze opened the door. Cynthia ran and grabbed a hold of his back for one last hug. She couldn't let him leave her house thinking she didn't love him. Blaze smiled as he felt his mother's embrace. The smile quickly disappeared when he saw what was waiting for him on the other end of the street.

Hood, Stacks, Tez-mo, Kevin and Piru patiently waited for Blaze to come out of his mother's house. Dressed in all black with blue flags tied tightly around their faces.

"I think the door unlocked, blood," Piru said.

"You sure?" Hood asked.

"I'm not positive, but I think so. Just be on point!" Piru answered.

"Nah, come on," Stacks ordered. All five men got up and took their position in the street in front of Ms. Harris house, each person ready to fire, each person ready to shoot and kill.

"You sure this how you want it, ock?" Hood asked Stacks. Stacks didn't reply. That was a good enough answer for him. The door opened suddenly and without hesitation the five men opened fire into the frame of the house, killing Blaze and Ms. Harris almost instantly. The gun fire stopped. Stacks looked at Piru and nodded. Piru took off toward the house with Tez-mo in tow. Blaze was dead. To make sure Blaze was really dead, Piru aimed and fired, hitting Blaze in his forehead. He did the same to Ms. Harris. Tez-mo dropped a blue flag on the face of Ms. Harris at the same time Piru dropped his on Blaze. The pair ran out the house and into the alley where their car awaited them.

***

Simfany slid through the house singing joyous Christmas tunes. The up-and-coming holiday was by far her favorite; the only thing missing was her baby boy. She no longer felt as if her back was against the wall. Carlos took claim of Jimdog, slowing him down. Even though his decision helped, she didn't understand his reasoning. But it was no longer her problem.

Moving out of Baltimore City to the county proved to be fruitful. She had a new best friend in Tijuana. They spent a lot of time together. At first their relationship was solely about Santana, but Simfany realized how lonely she really was. Having Tijuana and Carol in her corner was doing her some good. She even started back looking for a "Boo-Thing", as Tijuana's hot ass would call it. She didn't need or want hood niggas, though; she'd had her fair share of them.

As she sang along to "Jingle Bells", she was finishing up the touches on her dinner of fried chicken, corn on the cob, with mashed potatoes and gravy. Tijuana was on her way over for a girl's night in. They both needed a breather from all the stress they both were going through.

Awaiting Tijuana's arrival, Simfany got comfortable in the living room. Subconsciously, she curled up, tucking her feet under her. Simfany channel-searched, finding nothing worth watching, so she settled for a re-run of "The Wire" on HBO demand. She eventually drifted off to sleep.

Simfany was awakened by the light knocks on her door. Instinctively, she reached under the cushion for the gun that rested their twenty-four hours a day. She grabbed the 9-millimeter berretta and walked to the door, taking the safety off as she went. She looked through the peep hole only to see a smiling Tijuana. She put the safety back on, tucked the gun into her waist band, and opened the door. Tijuana walked inside shaking off the cold weather. They hugged. Tijuana took off her jacket and shoes as Simfany made her way back to the sofa. Tijuana sat in the love seat closest to the door.

"Who got killed out here?" Tijuana asked nosily.

"I don't know. Somebody got killed? Where?" Simfany asked, clueless herself. "When? Tonight?"

"That's what I heard. They actually said two people were killed."

"That's a damn shame," Simfany said, and added: "It should be on the news at eleven. We'll see what they talking about then." Tijuana nodded in agreement. Meanwhile they sat down and ate Simfany's favorite dish.

"Damn, girl, you did your thing with this chicken," Tijuana complimented as she bit into the golden crisp.

"Thank you, my Abuela showed me how to throw down." They both ate until they were full. Tijuana washed her dishes and reclaimed her seat back in the living room. Anxious to find out who got killed, she turned to the news channel ten minutes early, hoping she wouldn't miss anything. Simfany laughed. She'd never seen somebody so excited about murder. It was more to it than Simfany actually knew. She finished washing the remaining dishes, and then took her seat on the sofa. The eleven o'clock news was just coming on. The double homicide was the top story. Simfany and Tijuana listened to the reporter that was live at the scene.

"In what appears to be a gang hit, earlier this evening the lives of Narvel Harris and Cynthia Harris were cut short in a hail of gun fire. Narvel Harris, known to the streets as Blaze, was a star witness in the 2003 Murder case of Kane Moore, a known member of the

Shotgun Crip gang. Andre Jones was convicted of Moore's murder. Jones was also a known gang member. Mr. Harris skipped out months after his release, causing the state 's case to bend. It is believed that the Shotgun Crips put out a hit on Mr. Harris for his role in the death of Kane Moore. Evidence indicates the way the victims were found with blue bandanas across the face is associated with gang activity."

The last statement made Simfany's heart stop. When she was shot, a blue bandana was also dropped on her. Knowing that there might be a connection made Simfany uncomfortable.

Tijuana held her hands over her mouth in awe.

"What's wrong? I would think you would be happy." Simfany sat confused.

"They killed that boy's mother. That's wrong, Simfany, that's wrong." Tijuana cried for Cynthia's lost soul.

"I wanted revenge for my brother, but not like that. They killed his mother. An innocent person is dead because of Blaze's bitch ass." Simfany wanted to be able to feel the pain, but in all actuality she couldn't. She felt for Blaze's family though; they lost not one but two family members. Truthfully, her mind was stuck on the bandana situation. She knew in her gut, somehow, the bandanas were connected to her. It made her fearful, but with Carlos riding with her she didn't think nobody was stupid enough to come at her. She hoped not at least. Regardless, she would be ready this time.

Tijuana just sat there; it looked like she pulled the trigger herself. She was in some form of shock. Tijuana just sat there lost in her thoughts. Simfany gave Tijuana her space. A couple hours passed by and without words being spoke, it became awkward. Even though Simfany's own thoughts ran wild, her mood wasn't like Tijuana's. Tijuana seemed like she knew more about the deaths than she let on. Simfany could tell it was eating baby girl alive.

"Talk to me, T." Simfany broke the silence. "What's the matter? You been off into space for the last two hours. You okay?" Tijuana looked down at her hands and replied.

"Yeah, I'm good. It just fucks me up that, that lady had to die like that to satisfy my own hate."

"Oh, the way you looked, it's like you knew. If you know what I mean." Simfany hinted as she made her hand into a gun and pulled the trigger. Tijuana looked at Simfany, almost confirming her suspicions. *Fuck it! Shit happens,* Simfany thought. Something clicked though: *If Tijuana knows who killed Blaze and his mother, she would know who tried to kill me.* She began to fish.

"Who was it, T? You close to the niggas that killed that Narvel kid?" Tijuana said nothing. She just stared at the ceiling. But she managed to shake her head by way of saying, *No.*

"I don't know if the niggas I'm thinking about is responsible," Tijuana later answered.

"What you talking 'bout, ma?"

"About these blood niggas out here in Edgewood," Tijuana replied.

"Let me guess, Tree Top?"

"Yeah. But I don't know."

"What about them? They said blue flags, not red. I'm out of tune with all this gang shit but I know that bloods rock red," Simfany explained.

"I may be wrong, but there is no Crip niggas that fuck around in the Commons. The only people over there are the lor blood niggas. Not once did they say anything about a getaway car. They didn't have any witnesses. Right! Put two and two together. They gave Blaze a pass and told him to stay out of Edgewood. My only guess is he didn't. It's just sad that she lost her life too. That's the only thing really fucking with me. I thought it was two lor blood niggas that got torched. I feel responsible even if I didn't know. I watched the news every night hoping somebody would kill him for the sake of Kane. I would never have imagined that his mother would become a victim also."

"It's not your fault, ma." It was the only reassurance that Simfany could give. Tijuana would be fighting those demons she held for a long time. Simfany knew Tijuana would eventually be okay, truth being she had no choice but to get over it.

Knowing the little information that she did, she put two and two together and Tree Top Piru was a possible match. The conversation she had with Santana played through her thoughts like a movie. She couldn't remember if Santana said Blaze was affiliated with TTP or just blood. She would have to ask Santana without him worrying about her well-being.

Tijuana decided to spend the night because her mind wasn't all the way right. Plus, they were probably celebrating Blaze's demise in Washington Park. She couldn't be around that right now. The love that Tijuana received from her brother Kane, she thought, couldn't be replaced or equaled. She started to understand there was no need to replace, because the love Santana and Simfany showed her made her realize the love never left. It just came through different souls.

Santana and Simfany Vasquez, she smiled at the thought. Simfany left Tijuana downstairs to confront her demons. She particularly had something to do. Simfany grabbed a pen and a pad of paper. She wrote out a list of names; she connected the lines to each individual. She made side notes and why they may be connected. It was a must she get it right; her life depended on it. Simfany stayed up as long as her eyes allowed, connecting each player in her power circle.

One by one Harford County gang unit rounded up each member of TTP's blood gang in lieu of questioning for the murder of Narvel and Cynthia Harris. Each member denied involvement. With nowhere else for the gang unit to look, they kept a close eye on the gang. The hotline pointed to a particular sector of Edgewood but without more than a tip all they could do was wait, sit and watch.

Detective Ramos sat at his computer and looked over the new cases that eventually would float across his desk. Sub-consciously, he ran his hand across his forehead to wipe away the building sweat. The precinct was hot due to the winter air. It almost felt like hell. It was hot all year round in the precinct, especially when winter came around. Exhausted by the heat, he leaned back in his chair and took a break. *It's too early to feel this miserable.* He reached into his desk and grabbed the *Black and Mild's.* It was a way for him to concentrate at times. He needed his nicotine. He rose from his seat and went outside in the December weather. The breeze caught him immediately, cooling his body down. He was almost free to do whatever he wanted; it wouldn't last. Having no leads or suspects in the Vasquez case gave him ample amount of free time until a new case came through. How he looked at it, Simfany was a lost cause, she was one of those that didn't want any help and would end up dead because of the code of the streets.

Although his superior didn't know, it spelled vacation. Not the technical vacation, but extra leisure time. Ramos smoked his *Black and Mild* until he began to crave heat again. He put his cigar out and made his way back into the building. When Ramos returned to his desk, Lawson was posted at his desk feet up waiting on him. Ramos pushed his feet off the side, followed with a glare. Lawson smirked.

"Damn partner of mine. Why so angry?" Lawson laughed.

"Why you so happy, weirdo?" Ramos questioned.

"It's a beautiful morning." He sang the song from the Downy commercial. Ramos couldn't help himself; he had to laugh.

"You're silly. What's up? Everything you do there's a reason behind it. So, spill it."

"Read this." Lawson handed him the Baltimore Sun newspaper. Ramos looked at the bold print of the article.

"MOTHER AND SON SLAIN BY GANG HIT"

The words meant nothing to him; he didn't get it. The war between the Bloods and Crips was getting out of hand, but he didn't see the meaning of his partner's excitement. Tired of trying to decipher the article, he simply asked why?

"What am I supposed to see, Lawson?" Lawson's smiled faded; he reached out and grabbed the paper. He reached on to Ramos's desk and grabbed a highlighter. When detective Lawson handed the paper back, a half of a sentence was highlighted neon green. It stated:

"Narvel Blaze Harris and Cynthia Harris had blue flags draped across their faces when the police arrived at the scene. Indicating gang-"

Ramos shook his head. Clueless.

"Are you fucking kidding me? Ramos, the blue flags, they were dropped on the dead bodies as a symbol of some kind."

"So!"

"Simfany had the same blue flag *draped* on her when we arrived at her house." Lawson tried to express his urgency.

"And?" Ramos still didn't understand why it was so serious. It was a coincidence at its best.

"No shootings ever popped up with that type of symbol. That's the county thing, I'm guessing. This is connected big time. She may not be connected to the deceased, but the trigger man or men may be connected to her." It made sense to Lawson; he didn't understand some areas but it was something to look into. Ramos had to admit his partner was on to something.

"Impressive view, but now we must find the killer or killers to know our answer, right?" Ramos asked, genuinely confused. Lawson smiled.

"Wrong! Find the gang and start there. Connects bring answers, so when we start to connect the dots it's nowhere the bastards can hide." Lawson was ecstatic. This was a potential huge deal. His hunches told him Carlos somehow plays a major role. Only if he knew for sure, he could bring Carlos's empire down by a mere fuck up which would mean a big promotion. It wasn't about Simfany anymore or her getting justice. It was now about the people involved, and now it was about his own future.

Chapter Eight

"Even though you haven't been the best possible inmate, you always remain respectful to the staff in my building. You're young, Mr. Vasquez, do something with your life besides this," Mr. Donahue stated as he used his arms to make his point. He continued: "If being in jail forever is what you want, they will always have a cell to house you. I say that to say this, I think you 're ready to go home. You have a good support system out there; this can be left behind you. I will be signing the papers for your completion of this program in the next couple of days. Please stay out of trouble and stay out of prison. Whenever your probation officer can set you a date in court, you will be released. Good luck." Donahue reached out his hand and gave Santana a strong handshake. Santana was ecstatic. Going home was the last thing he had on his mind when he was called to his monthly review. Mr. Donahue was the unit manager of King Hall, and rarely was he seen. When he did show his face, it was usually bad news. Santana remained still; his thoughts had wondered beyond the gates of The Charles H. Hickey School.

"Lor yo!" Drew called as he looked into the office. That snapped Santana out of his momentary phase. Drew was smiling ear to ear.

"Damn, that nigga told people already?" Santana smiled.

"Shorty, what are you talking about?" Drew's smile faded with a newfound confusion.

"Donahue didn't tell you? Oh, shit, he didn't.

"Nigga, what are you talking about?" Santana smiled.

"He signed my release papers, my G!" Santana said in excitement, and a smile even bigger now was plastered Drew's face.

"Damn, lor yo, 'bout time they let you go. I'm gone miss ya high yellow ass when you leave. I had my shot and fucked up. Be safe and stay out. Ya mom need you. When you leave?" Drew asked him. Santana shrugged.

"You be gone soon but look though—they killed the nigga Blaze last night, and they killed his mother too," Drew said in a whisper. Santana caught the last part for what it was. He couldn't imagine putting his mother in a situation to cause her death, especially a situation that could and should have been avoided. He didn't realize it, but he was still seated in Donahue's office. Drew mentioned it and he got up and left, shutting the door to its frame. *Damn, that's ruthless—the nigga's mom though,* Santana thought as he was making his way out the door. He couldn't stoop that low. *I would've burned Blaze, no problem, but his mother, not happening.*

Knowing Tijuana, she wouldn't like the news either. There was nothing exciting about the tragedy. But he kept his comment to himself and walked to his cell. Santana laid down in his bed. He almost let the news about Blaze take his shine. Going home to his mother was more important at this point. He tucked his hands behind his head and contemplated on his release. What Mr. Donahue said about coming back stuck to his brain. How he saw it was, sometimes you didn't have a choice whether you will come back or stay out. The only difference was Santana had the choice right now, but his mind was made. The war started way before he stepped foot into Baltimore City. And with his mother's blood being shed, niggas had to answer for it. What bothered him was going against an enemy he didn't know existed.

He didn't know who to come at, but he vowed to play his cards right and get even. If his consequences were incarceration, so be it; regardless, he was prepared. His thought ran extreme at this point, but he was well aware of his intentions. Santana sat up and left his room. He was so happy he didn't know if he wanted to chill or move around. As he made his way up the steps to the multipurpose room, a thought crossed his mind. He stopped at the counselor's office on the way up the steps; he knocked and waited for a response. When he got one, he poked his head into the door.

"What's up?" Ms. Jackson asked behind her desk.

"Can I get a lawyer call, Ms. J?" Her desk was full of monthly reviews, so it was a 50/50 chance she would say yes.

"Give me a second to clean this shit up and I got you. You can sit down if you want."

Santana made his way into the spacious office and took the nearest seat to him. He watched as Ms. Jackson tried to clear her desk. There were papers everywhere. It was hard not to stare at her also. She was beautiful and shapely. The only thing that was unattractive about the lady was, she was too hood at heart, and very unorganized. She was an around-the-way girl, but beautiful none the less. Santana played with his hair as she finished clearing her desk. Sometimes, he didn't understand certain things about her; there were two brand new file cabinets lined against the wall, but she never used them. He shrugged. *Oh well.*

"Come on, Tana. Who you calling again?" Ms. Jackson asked.

"My lawyer. I gotta have him get me a court date ASAP."

"Oh, shit, they did sign your release today with your bad ass." She smiled, showing her gold fangs to the world. The girl was beautiful. "Bout time they let you go. What's the number?" she asked with the dial tone humming through the speakers.

"443-555-9624." The phone rand for about twenty seconds before Rick picked up.

"Rick Holliver—how I may help you?" he yelled through the speaker. Santana grabbed the receiver and explained the events of the day. He took notice of his lawyer's happiness, with a promise to tell his mother and get a court date as soon as possible, then Rick was gone. Santana replaced the receiver back into its cradle and stood. He thanked Ms. Jackson and left the office.

There were still no leads in the double homicide that took place in Edgewood; the city was quiet. With the police on hunt missions for any gang activity, Hood Ru and Stacks stayed low under the radar. Stacks had no clue, but Hood was fucked up over killing Cynthia. Hood knew what he signed up for, just like the rest of them did, especially Blaze. What's done is done; there was nothing Hood could really do about it. He just knew if a similar situation arose again, it would be much different. His main objective right now was to stay out of jail, especially for a role in a double homicide.

Jamel Mitchell

Chapter Nine

It was barely above 30 degrees, and the sun was out as Santana exited Mitchell Courthouse with Simfany and Pretty Ricky in tow. He
was finally free. Santana took a deep breath. The cold air rushed
into his body. *Freedom is bliss*, he thought. Santana turned around
to face his mother and lawyer. They both smiled. Santana laughed
at their corniness.

"Y'all niggas is corny, standing there looking like proud par-
ents." Saying it shot a dagger into his heart. He shook his head off
as he tried to push the thought of his father away.

"So, you think you got jokes?" Simfany glared at her son.

"Nah, pretty lady, I was just joking." Santana walked up to his
mother and hugged her.

"There is a lot we need to talk about," she whispered into his
ear. They held their embrace for a second. Santana held out his hand
to his lawyer; Rick gripped it and shook it with an ounce of pride.

"Without you this probably wouldn't be possible. I fucked up a
lot, but you still fought for me, thank you. I don't know if the money
made you do the things you did, but whatever the motive I appreciate it." Santana looked into Rick Holliver's eyes.

"At first it was about the money, but the loyalty you have for
your mother made me realize something else. Money means nothing
without family and someone to share it with. Plus, she really needs
you out here. Try to stay out of trouble, Santana. Please." Santana
nodded in agreement.

"Make sure you stay in constant contact with your Probation
Officer. He's an okay individual, to be honest. So, if you fuck up,
it's definitely your fault. As long as you don't get any new charges,
he could care less. I have another hearing in the next thirty minutes
or so. You be safe for one and stay out of trouble. *Call me if you
need me*." He looked at Simfany for the last part of that statement."
Rick nodded, turned and walked back into the courthouse.

"Come on, Santana, we going home. It's cold as a bitch out
here. Santana walked side by side with Simfany through downtown
Baltimore to a 24-hour parking garage. The sights were similar,

only this time he wasn't handcuffed and shackled looking through a cage window. They waited as the garage worker went and found Simfany's truck. *Damn, ma Duke is doing it big,* he thought as the Tahoe whipped around the bend. It was a nice car. Simultaneously they hoped in. It felt good to be back with his mother. He took his coat off and sat on the back seat. Santana adjusted his seat and leaned back. He took the rubber band out of his hair to let his hair breathe, got comfortable and fell asleep.

It had been a long day, so Simfany expected it sometime today that Santana would get exhausted. She wanted and needed to talk to Santana about the bandana situation and the web she made up. As she looked over at her son. He was sound asleep. She knew she would wait until a later date to discuss her issue. Simfany was just glad to see her baby back home where he needed to be. She reached for the radio and turned it to 92Q. Jagged Edge was playing on the radio. Simfany remembered the song was called *"Good Luck Charm"*. She turned the volume down to a soft whisper and continued her drive home.

It was a 45-minute drive from Baltimore City to Edgewood. Santana slept the whole way. Simfany pulled up in front of her town house. She nudged Santana to wake up. He stirred, and then stretched. He was tired from the previous night. The anxiety of getting out kept him awake. He gathered his coat and hopped out the car. The cold air hit him; without his coat on, the air was unbearable. He quickly ran up the small lawn and into the house. *Damn,* he thought as he shivered. Santana walked straight to the kitchen and opened the refrigerator.

"Aww, hell no! Nigga, if you don't get your ass in here!" Simfany yelled from the stairs. Santana walked to the steps to see what his mother was yelling about.

"Take them dusty ass shoes off when you walk through here. No shoes, Santana, wall-to-wall carpet. Now take them shoes off." Santana looked at his mother and gave her the *you- showing-your-ass* look. But he did what he was told and took his shoes off.

"My fault I didn't pay attention to your 'wall-to-wall' carpeting." He made quotation marks with his fingers. Simfany playfully swung; Santana dipped her slap and ran. Simfany smirked. She was happy her son was home.

What he missed most was eating, so he made that his first priority. He pulled out shrimps, chicken, and a slab of T-bone steak. He couldn't decide what he wanted to eat, so he chose all three. After eating that jail food for the last two-plus years, he craved the items. Santana sat the steak under cold water to thaw out; he put the chicken and shrimps in separate bowls to also thaw. Being free felt good. He had forgotten the feeling of doing what you wanted to do; it felt weird to a certain point. As he looked for the seasoning in the cabinet, Simfany was making her way into the kitchen in a pair of sweats and a t-shirt. When she saw the water run, and the food laid out, she knew Santana had a big meal in mind. The boy was in a beast in the kitchen, almost better than her. But if anybody would ever argue, she would beg to differ.

She was excited to be back around him. She just sat and admired his swag; he was just like his father. *Damn, that boy hair is long as hell,* she thought. She watched as Santana struggled to reach a bowl in the cabinet; she got up out her seat to help him. At first it startled him because he wasn't used to someone touching his back.

"Move, boy, so I can get the bowl," she stated. Obediently, he moved out of the way. Simfany grabbed the bowl and set it on the table. He reached into the bottom cabinet and grabbed the flour. Everything but the steak was going to be fried.

"What are you making?" Simfany asked.

"Everything, anything I dreamed about on all those long nights, I'm trying to eat 'em all. Right now, I'm thinking fried chicken like Abuela used to make, maybe a little shrimp and a medium rare steak with a salad and mashed potatoes." He opened the refrigerator and took two eggs out of a carton. The egg was used as a special batter for the chicken. In awe Simfany watched her son at work. Being locked up didn't take from his culinary skills.

"What's up though, ma? You're sitting there all quiet. You making a nigga nervous." He laughed, but he was serious.

"I just can't believe I got you back. You're all grown up now. You got a little mustache and everything. A light-skinned version of ya father, except your hair is extremely long. What are you doing with it? I only ask because my braiding days are over. That shit too long for me to fuck with."

"I just probably keep it in a ponytail until I can find somebody that *wants* to do my hair." His long thick but silky hair ran down to the top of his rib cage. He was fifteen years old and never had a haircut, and he wasn't planning on one for a while. He changed the subject.

"I remember you said you needed to talk to me. I think I know what about too, but there's no telling. So, what's up?" He sat across from his mother and played with his hair.

"I can wait," Simfany replied nonchalantly as if the conversation was of no importance. She really didn't want to put the situation out there because she didn't know if she was tripping or not. But if they were going to stay and live in Maryland, it was a must they speak on it.

"Nah, I'm good. No secrets, remember. I'm grown, ma, talk to me." She couldn't argue the fact that he turned from a young boy into a thorough young man. The situation's he been through made him age faster than his years.

"It's about when I got shot. There are a couple of things that I put together as far as connections may go." Santana's eyes widened. This was the conversation he hoped they would be having. He wanted revenge. He would shed blood through whatever city to get right with what happened to his lady. He would life for his mother. Nothing more needed to be said because Simfany knew what it was. He was attentive as he listened to her theory. She explained the possible connection between the blue bandanas being dropped at the scenes. She gave him the rundown on the web she made on what connected everyone. None of the knowledge meant anything official, but it created a visual of what happened and possibly how she was dragged into the madness. Santana cooked and listened.

"But to be honest, I want to go back home," she said.

"Why?" he asked as he dropped another chicken wing into the hot grease. She watched him stir the chicken around before she answered.

"I say that because we can avoid all of the bullshit that comes with living here. We can go back home or somewhere else and live comfortably. I got the money to get us straight. I got more than enough money to live happily. We wouldn't want for nothing. Don't get me wrong, living here was okay but the drama is too much. If I wanted you to grow up like this I would have stayed in Melrose."

"I feel you, but you got holes in ya body from a nigga walking these streets. Daddy wouldn't want that nigga to have the luxury. So, I beg you, pretty lady, let me handle this, and to be honest there is nothing to go back to New York for. Both my friends are dead. One killed the other for unknown reasons, Lonnie is dead mentally. What's the point? We good here." He walked over to where she was sitting and kissed his mother on her forehead.

"I love you, Santana, very much, and I'm not trying to bury my son. I can't take what Lonnie went through. I just can't." Her eyes watered. She was on the verge of breaking down, thinking about the possibility of Santana meeting an early grave.

"When it's my time, you or I can't stop it and we both know that. But I'm good." He turned and took a golden piece of chicken out the pot and sat it in a basket on the countertop.

"And for the record, I'll let my body turn cold any day for you." At that point he stood in front of her as she looked up. Her eyes still were watery. He wiped the forming tear away.

"Please don't cry, ma. We good, I promise. Stop worrying before our hair fall out." He made an attempt to cheer her up. She smiled and wiped her eyes. He was right. She realized there was nothing else that needed to be said about the issue. Now that he was home another thing crossed her mind: Tijuana. Tijuana had a lot of love for Santana, but at times she didn't know what kind. It really didn't bother her; but Simfany had to see if the attraction was mutual.

"Let me ask you a question, how you feel about Tijuana? I mean in a literal sense as far as girlfriend type shit." Santana ignored her. He focused on his task at hand. He reached into the cabinet and got the remaining mashed potatoes. He read the box and started to get ready to cook them.

"Nigga, you keep ignoring me and I'm gone pop you in ya mouth," she said playfully. Still, he let the previous question go unanswered.

"Santana Vasquez!" she yelled. He looked at her.

"What, ma?" he finally answered.

·"Do you like the girl or what?"

Lying through his teeth, he answered: "That's my nigga, nothing more, nothing less. I fuck with shorty hard body." He always had a crush on Tijuana, but knowing it would never be nothing, he played the brother and sister role with her. And even though at times he viewed her as a sister he knew she was not.

"Okay. I was just asking. But you know what's kind of funny? Y'all both say the same shit with the same stupid ass looks on your faces. But if you say so." She saw right through him. She promised herself she would stay out of their business. If it was meant to be, then it would be. Santana had finally finished cooking lunch for himself and his mother. He made both plates then served Simfany.

"Pretty lady," he said as he slid her plate in front of her.

"I can get used to this," she cheesed. He smiled and sat down. They said grace and dug in. The words were exchanged earlier, so not much was said as they smashed the meals in front of them.

Simfany took responsibility over the dishes, while Santana went upstairs to shower. It had amazed Simfany how fast Santana grew up. She remembered as if it was yesterday when he ran back to Dracula's grave to lay his birthday necklace there for his father. She also realized she would no longer be the only female in his life. Marissa was his first love, from Melrose, but he wasn't connected to her like he used to be. Now it was a different story. She knew she would forever hold the number one spot. Simfany was so lost in her thoughts she didn't hear Santana call out to her until the second time.

"Ma!" he called again.

"What's up?" she replied as she walked into the living room.

"I'm about to go to the store. You want anything?" He stood with the door open.

"Yeah but close the damn door. It's freezing. Get me a regular Dutch." She walked back into the kitchen. She heard the door slam, indicating Santana's departure. Santana walked through Meadowood by memory. The funny part was: he never stepped foot in the complex, but the story Drew told gave him a vivid picture. The short cut to the *Shell* station was the most visual. Drew explained about shootings, and stabbings taking place in the cut at night. As he took the path through the cut, he looked up noticing the gas station was only about fifty yards away. It really wasn't that far. The day light was still shining, and he instinctively took in his surroundings. The cut looked like an old basketball court that went without lawn care for years. It didn't look as menacing as the stories would tell, but when nightfall came, the dangers increased by a large margin. He walked and looked. The trees shielded a view from the apartment windows from either side of the complex. No streetlight was equipped anywhere close. The only potential light was the gas station at the end of the trail. The *Shell* gas station sat on Hanson Road; it was the same place where Blaze got arrested the night Kane was killed. His thoughts ran wild. *Tijuana's brother would have never liked me.* He could feel it in his bones, but he would never know. It was too late; his opinion no longer mattered. The brisk air made Santana pull his skully down over his ears and speed up his pace.

Santana arrived at the store in a matter of minutes. Still shaking off the chill of the afternoon as he entered the store, he didn't pay attention to the female departing. He bumped into her, causing her to drop the bags she held. He bent down to help pick up the contents and realized he had broken her eggs. The girl looked as if she really wanted to cry.

"My bad, ma. Whatever I fucked up I'll pay for," Santana said sincerely.

"Nah, you're okay. I saw you coming. I should of moved out the way." On the one hand, he didn't notice because his head was down as he entered the store. She, on the other hand, was a different story. She stood mesmerized by his presence. She would never admit it, but it was definitely her fault that they ran into each other.

"Please ma, I got you. It ain't shit for real." He pulled a ten dollar bill out the stack of money his Simfany gave him. He reached out to hand her the money. She reluctantly accepted it. He was glad because he wouldn't have taken no for an answer.

"So, beautiful, what's ya name?"

"Paris," she replied as her face turned a bright red. "Thank you for the money," she added.

"Oh, shit, you good. That was my fault anyway." As the two exchanged pleasantries, in walked another customer. Santana and Paris were blocking the doorway so the person entering the store had no choice but to speak.

"Excuse me, homie," the boy said polite as possible, not trying to cause no unwanted attention. Santana turned around immediately.

"My bad, my G," Santana replied and moved out the way, letting the dude pass. The boy nodded.

"Good looking, homie. What's good, Paris? Long time no see." He stopped a second to acknowledge Paris.

"Hi, Piru." She smiled. When Piru walked off, she rolled her eyes. Santana shook his head and laughed at her fake smile.

"A'ight, ma, you be safe," Santana said before passing her.

"You too," she replied. His thought process was now somewhere else. The boy's name alone gave Santana mixed feelings. As he got the junk food he wanted, he eyed Piru, remembering his face. Everything else he would recognize as far as height and weight. Damn near everybody was taller than him. And the dreads he had was a dead giveaway. He put Piru in his memory banks.

After gathering everything he came for, he went to the cash register, ready to leave. Piru waited patiently behind him. Paris waved goodbye as she left. Santana was next in line.

"Is that it?" the clerk asked.

"Nah, let me get a box of Dutches too, please, and thank you." The clerk looked at Santana for recognition but came up blank. "You got ID?" the clerk asked.

"Nah, but I'm eighteen." Santana tried.

"I can understand that, but no ID—no cigar. Sorry, my friend."

For the Love of Blood 2

"That's cool, just ring this up for me then," Santana said, handing him the food he picked out. After his groceries were paid for, he grabbed his bag and departed. He bundled up for the awaiting cold air. He started his way back through the path.

"Yo, blood!" was all Santana heard, but he still didn't turn around.

"Yo, shorty!" Santana recognized the voice as Piru's. He didn't understand why he was calling him so he turned around in a defense manner. Piru was jogging to him with a box in his hands.

"What's poppin, my G?" Santana asked as Piru approached.

"That five, shorty. But I got them blunts for you. Mike act like that if he don't know you. You bang, homie?" Piru had to ask by the way Santana greeted him.

"Nah, a lot of my niggas pop five though. Anyway, good looking on them blunts. How much the box cost? I—" His words were cut short.

"You good, homie, just take care of yourself. I'm gone. Hold up. Before I bounce, shorty, what's ya name, homie?"

"Santana."

"Piru, TTP 400 block Spruce. Good to meet you, homie. Be safe out here, my nigga." Just as fast as Piru ran up, he left. Santana watched him jog back to the *Shell* station and hop in the passenger side of a car. The car pulled off instantly. Santana continued on his way back home. He made it to the end of the block about to cross the street when he saw the car Piru hopped in driving down the hill. His heart pace quickened. Santana wanted to run, but he held his composure. As the car flew past, the horn beeped twice. Santana sighed; his paranoia got the best of him. But to make sure he wasn't still there if they passed again, he hurried across the street to his home.

Heart racing as the door closed, he took his shoes off, put his bags down and looked out the front window. He watched the movement around the house for five minutes. When he realized nobody was watching him, he went into the kitchen and unloaded the small bag of groceries. Santana put Simfany's Dutch Master Cigars on the glass table in the living room and went upstairs to calm his own nerves by working out, one of his daily routines since being incarcerated.

Hood speed down Meadowood Drive; he swung a quick left on: his way to Candlewood Court. The court was a death zone. It was one way in, one way out. Candlewood was where all the bullshit took place; it was known for its violence. If you weren't welcomed there, you would know it.

"Who was young bull you had me beep at? Bull hair was long as shit too. That's crazy."

He made a right turning into the Candlewood. He slowed the car for speed bumps as he waited for Piru's response.

"Some lor homie I just met in the Shell. The lor nigga greeted me like, *'What's poppin' my G'*. I know right, the antennas went up. He said all his niggas back home blood." Piru explained as he licked the Dutch in his hand.

"He's a New York nigga then, my young bull in Philly from that way and that's all he says is *my G*!" Hood laughed as he parked.

"What's the niggas name?" Hood asked, pulling his seat to a recline. Piru thought about it for a second. He finished rolling the blunt and passed it to Hood.

"I'm burnt. I forgot that fast." He had it on the end of his tongue but couldn't quite remember. "Man, what's the nigga name that signed with them Harlem niggas? You know who I'm talking about. The lor Dominican nigga that always got that bandanna on?" Piru got frustrated and quit trying. Hood didn't know what the fuck he was talking about. Hood used the car lighter to light the blunt. He pulled on the blunt, filling his lungs with smoke. The name came to him as he exhaled.

"You talking about the bull Juelz Santana?" Hood asked.

"Yeah, lor homie name is Santana. The young niggas name is Santana." Piru reached out and grabbed the blunt from Hood.

Santana—Santana—where have I heard that name from before? Hood thought deeply.

He searched his mind but came up blank. The two sat and got baked. Piru was reclined on his phone when the thought came to Hood who Santana was.

"Oh shit, ock." Hood jumped up. Piru reached for his gun.

"What's poppin', homie?" Piru looked around, ready for war.

"The nigga Santana the young bull that almost killed Blaze in hickey. It was him and the lor nigga Drew, and I think the Rican broad his moms. I hear the young nigga got heart!" Hood Ru admitted. Nobody else knew about Stacks shooting Simfany, but him. His reaction was out of pure amazement on how small the world was. If the lor nigga was a goon like everybody said he was, he wouldn't mind having him on his team. As long as he didn't find out about his mother, he would be straight. But if Hood saw any sign of recognition in his eyes, Hood wouldn't hesitate to body the young boy. After realizing there was no imminent danger, Piru put his gun back on his lap. Piru pulled out another Dutch and his smoke sack. They both needed another session to calm their nerves. *Fuck that nigga Blaze,* Piru thought to himself as he rolled yet another blunt.

Due to the fact that Santana took classes while he was at his multiple placements, the credits followed. Instead of being in the 8th grade where he left off, his credits he earned put him in his regular grade the 10th. He went to Joppatowne High School; it was fifteen minutes away from home. Everybody that lived in Edgewood in the Meadowood sector along Hanson Road attended Joppatowne High School. The school was big and the fan base was extreme. The basketball games were damn near sold out every home game for both JV and varsity. During the day it was all work no play, but just like every school there were problems. The growing problem at Joppatowne was the gangs and cliqued up squads. The school system tried to solve the problem by having a police officer on duty at all times. The police officer's name was Mr. Gregg. He was a bald man with glasses that tolerated no nonsense. He ran the school as he saw fit.

Santana started school in the middle of the school year, with no friends besides Paris and Piru. He had no obligations besides school, so he stayed to himself and did what was asked of him. He was popular amongst the females, and generally hated by the male gender because of that.

It wasn't nothing new to Santana. He was used to the envy, so he played it cool. Santana was tested on many occasions and let niggas live, but incident after incident started to happen so he promised himself that the next person that acted stupid was gone get it. And that situation arose sooner than he expected. As Santana sat at the table with Paris, Jason walked past and bumped him.

"Excuse yourself, my nigga!" Santana said as he looked back. Jason kept walking. Paris saw the flame that rested behind his eyes. Santana promised Simfany that he would do his best to stay out of trouble, but it seemed like when he wasn't on his bullshit, trouble found him. Santana was pissed how niggas kept trying him. The motto he followed in Hickey he tried to let go, but as he let each nigga slide, the next person came harder at him. As he sat there and contemplated, he decided that today would be the last time a person would come out his mouth sideways.

"Calm down, Santana, that nigga wack. He is not worth you getting suspended over," Paris said, trying to calm him down.

"Ma, you don't understand, these niggas think I'm pussy for some odd reason or another. I'm good, but I swear on my life today the last day a nigga gone disrespect me. I don't give a fuck who it is. True story." He meant every word. Paris had just braided his hair days earlier. He braided the ends and tucked them into his shirt so his hair wouldn't be grabbed and pulled. So, gone to his thoughts, he didn't see Piru walk up to the table.

"Lor homie, you good? You look like you got a nigga on the menu." Piru recognized the look. He looked at Paris, and she shrugged. Piru tapped Santana. He looked up into a familiar face. The only nigga he halfway knew.

"You good, blood?" Piru asked again. Santana explained the situation to him that dated back a couple of weeks. He also explained why he let go and let niggas live. Piru understood but wanted to know what was on his mind.

"I'm gone holla at the nigga. One wrong word—I'm gone smash son." Paris just sat there and said nothing. It was nothing that could change his mind, and she knew he wasn't totally wrong for feeling that way. She witnessed the hating with her own eyes. She remained quiet. There was nothing she could say. Paris looked up and shook her head as she made eye contact with a smiling Jason.

Paris shook her head. *Damn,* she thought as Jason made his way to them with his lunch tray. She looked at Santana, then looked past him to signal Jason's presence. Santana turned to see Jason walking toward him with a smug grin on his face. Santana took off his Nike book bag and stood. Out the corner of his eyes he saw Piru tying up his dreads.

He reached his right arm out to tap Piru. Piru stopped and looked up. Santana shook his head by way of saying no, because win, lose, or draw—these niggas was gone respect him. Piru nodded in respect. Santana's attention reverted back to Jason. They mugged each other as Jason walked up to the table towards Santana, Piru and Paris, and sat down. *This nigga think he funny,* Jason laughed to himself.

"My nigga why you keep trying to play me like I'm some kind of swine or something?" Santana asked calmly.

"Swine? Fuck is you talking 'bout, lor nigga?" He laughed, trying to impress Paris. Santana looked over at Paris.

"No disrespect, ma." He looked back to Jason. "Trying to impress for some pussy gone get you hurt, my G. Yeah, Paris beautiful, but understand this: you won't bag her off my expense. You keep playing with me and I'm gone burn your hoe ass." Santana stepped closer. The smile that was once on Jason's face disappeared.

"Nigga, who the fuck you think you talking to?" Jason replied. Santana inched closer until they were face to face, eye to eye.

"No more needs to be said then!" Santana said as he raised his voice.

"Nigga, you know what?" Jason attempted to stand. Santana wasted no time and leaned into him, dropping Jason backwards off the bench. Santana rushed him, hitting him three-more times in the side of the head. Jason stumbled over the seats as he tried to run from Santana.

Santana didn't let up until Piru grabbed his arm.

"You did you, my nigga. Come on!" Piru said as he tried to pull him away from a crumbled Jason. Santana saw four people approaching out the corner of his eye. The pace of his heart quickened. He recognized them as people that Jason hung around with on a daily basis. Santana shrugged out of his friend's grip and waited on the attack.

"What's poppin, bitch ass niggas!" Santana yelled. The four moved closer, trying to surround him.

"Hold up, blood, what y'all nigga think y'all doing?" Piru asked angrily. None of them answered. "A'ight, since none of you niggas wanna answer, let me put it to you like this, any one of you touch my lor homie I'm gone smoke you. That's on my muthafuckin momma, nigga!" Piru stated venomously. His reputation proceeded himself. Piru was known around Harford County to let his gun ring, not just for show either. Piru was a loose cannon. The threat didn't fall on deaf ears. To show how much he wasn't playing, he moved out the way, leaving Santana solo in the middle of the cafeteria. Nobody moved. They weren't trying to take it there. Santana chuckled.

"Son, you niggas are really hoes," Santana said as he grabbed his Nike bag. Paris had her hand over her mouth as the three left out the cafeteria.

As soon as the trio reached the hallway, Mr. Gregg came running around the corner with his taser gun extended.

"Get on the ground, Mr. Vasquez, Mr. Mayfield—now!" he yelled. They both lay on the floor awaiting further instruction. Santana shook his head in disappointment; he knew he was most likely going back to Hickey. They were cuffed and escorted to the principal's office. Mr. Gregg went into the principal's office and came back out within minutes. He uncuffed Piru and told him to go to his next period class. He also uncuffed Santana but told him to remain seated.

Santana was suspended from school for ten days. He could care less. It was disappointing his mother that bothered him. But he knew she would understand, so he really wasn't sweating it. On the bus ride home Paris sat next to Santana. She admitted to how she felt about him, only to find that his feelings were mutual. He explained enough of his past for her to understand him better. He also wanted her to make the decision off of knowing him instead of his looks. Paris didn't care, as long as he promised to respect her and never to raise his hands to her. He kissed Paris in agreement.

Chapter Ten

Simfany had to get out of the house. She been cooped up since Santana had gotten home. Besides shopping for food, she rarely left her home. *I gotta do something or I'm gone go crazy in here,* she told herself. She got dressed; the grey *Banana Republic* jeans she chose to wear fit Simfany' s body like a glove. Simfany looked at herself in the mirror. *Damn, a bitch still got it.* She twisted and twirled, checking out her own body. She reached into her closet and pulled out a grey matching Coogi sweater.

Simfany made her way down the stairs. She looked over at Paris. Paris was laid across the couch with her head in Santana's lap fast asleep. Santana sat bare chest, playing with Paris's hair.

The two made a cute couple, Simfany had to admit. But she was still vexed at Santana for getting suspended a couple weeks back. She locked eyes with Santana as she made her way down the stairs. She was still disappointed. Simfany walked lightly over to Santana in hopes of not waking Paris.

Simfany whispered: "I'm going shopping. The Glock is in the box, but please stay out of trouble." She leaned over and kissed him on the cheek. She grabbed her coat and left. Simfany walked the short distance down the hill to her truck. She opened the door and placed her purse in the passenger seat before she climbed in. Before she pulled off, Simfany pulled the gun out of her purse and placed it in the divider for safe measures. It was more so routine than anything. She pulled out of Meadowood, eyes set on going to White Marsh Mall to buy her and Santana something nice.

As Simfany pulled out of the complex, a Maroon Crown Vic followed. Piru pulled up to the double twin town house and beeped the horn. He turned the volume down inside the car and waited for Santana to come outside. As he waited, he made himself useful; he reached into the glove compartment and pullet out the box of already rolled blunts. He searched his Dickies for the lighter he purchased only hours earlier. But Piru couldn't find it. *Fuck!* he yelled. He was frustrated. The rental he had come equipped with no car lighter; he was stuck. He reached back into his pocket and pulled out his cell phone and dialed Santana's number from memory. The phone was picked up in two rings by the voicemail. He redialed the number again. This time he was sent straight to voicemail. Piru redialed again. The caller answered.

"Nigga, what?" Santana called from the other end of the phone.

"Lor nigga, bring a lighter with you when you come out," Piru replied.

"Nah, nigga, bring ya lazy ass inside!" Santana hung up the phone. Piru took the keys out of the ignition and got out the car. He walked the short distance to the door, he opened the door and walked in. *Damn, this shit laid out in here,* he thought to himself as he looked around. Paris came out the kitchen laughing with Santana in tow. They both stopped suddenly when they noticed Piru staring.

"Take ya shoes off before you come over here. Mom Dukes be trippin. She would fuck both of us up!" Santana stated. Piru kicked off his Nike boots at the door and made his way through the living room into the kitchen. He passed the two love birds and lit the blunt in his mouth.

"That's all you do—Smoke!" Paris said in the doorway of the kitchen.

"So what? All you wanna do is be under my lor nigga all day," he teased back.

"Fuck you, Patrick." She laughed because she knew he wasn't lying.

"Damn, that's how you feel, lor homie?" He sucked his teeth and shook his head. "That's alright with ya big forehead having ass!" Piru snapped back.

"Whatever, Patrick, you bet not get my baby into no trouble with ya crazy ass. I mean that shit, Piru." Paris was dead serious.

"He safe with me and you know that" he reassured.

"I said trouble, Piru, *trouble*. Keep him out of trouble. Please!" Paris said sternly. Santana laughed at them. They were too much sometimes.

"Fuck you laughing at, Blood? You set me up for this shit too, nigga. You ain't funny. Hurry up, I 'm going to smoke in the car."

Santana nodded. Piru made his way out the door. He looked at Paris. Paris smiled.

"Be safe with him; he stay into some shit," she warned.

"I'll be alright, ma. You just worry about keeping that thing wet for a nigga until I get back." Santana leaned in and kissed her passionately.

"I will, sexy, you just remember what I said." She stepped on her tip toes and kissed him again.

"A'ight, ma, I gotta go. I'll call you later." He kissed her forehead then ran out the house. It was hard to leave her, but he wanted to chill with his nigga. He ran out the door with his timbs in one hand and his flight jacket in the other. The passenger door came open as he ran down the hill to the parking lot. Santana hoped in and closed the door. The couple of seconds it took him to get inside the car, the cold air chilled his body. "Nigga, turn the heat on and pass the weed," Santana said as he shivered. Piru looked at Santana like he was crazy, but he cut the heat on and passed Santana the box of already rolled blunts. Santana looked at the box then at Piru.

"Really, homie you think I would lace you?" Piru asked seriously. Santana took his comment to heart and went against his better judgment. He reached for the lighter he had in his pants and lit one of the pre-rolled Dutches.

Piru pulled out of the driveway and left Meadowood.

"Where we 'bout to go, big homie?" Santana asked.

"I'm 'bout to take you to my stomping ground—*The Commons*," he replied. Santana knew *The Commons* was known for gang activity and violence. He also knew that was where Blaze got bodied.

"Cool with me," Santana replied.

"I want you to meet my fam; they heard a lot about you and wanna meet you," Piru explained as he passed Beacon Terrace, making a sharp right into Harford Commons. Santana subconsciously checked his hip. The Glock his mother gave him was there. He was nervous. He knew Piru, but the rest of them TTP niggas he didn't know. He was taught to always be on point no matter the situation, and he was.

Off first glance you would have thought *The Commons* was a pretty nice neighborhood because of how the row houses were set up and the lawn care. Santana knew it looked pleasant in the day but turned deadly at night. He relaxed and waited for the ride to end. Santana was too high by the time Piru pulled up in front of a white compacted looking house. He opened the ashtray and put the remainder of the blunt inside.

"Come on, homie, we here," Piru said as he got out the car and dusted himself off. Santana sighed. *Do or die,* he thought. He exited the car behind Piru and followed him inside the house.

When Santana walked into the house, a cloud of smoke rushed out into the cold air. Santana watched as Piru made his way through the living room, throwing up signature handshakes to all his brethren. He admired the love that Piru was shown. It brought back memories of when he was back home. Piru broke the silence.

"Yo, blood, this my lor nigga Tana I been telling y'all about. Homie a goon by all right." Santana walked through the house, meeting and slapping everybody up. Each face he saw he added to his memory bank. Even though he felt the love, none of the seven individuals he could trust. It was a possibility that the nigga that shot his mom was present. He had to play his part. He couldn't show no ill hatred to anybody, or they would catch on to his ulterior motive. It was smart of him because Hood Ru was in the far corner observing his posture.

"Sit down, lor nigga, you good. This my familia." Piru held out the blunt box for Santana. He declined. He was already slipping. He needed to be on point as much as possible. His life may depend on it. He watched as two people played the new 2005 NBA Live, so he didn't see Hood creep up on him. Hood stood next to Santana for a minute without acknowledging himself. Santana never looked back, so Hood tapped his shoulder. He waited to see his reaction; to his surprise, all Santana did was look up at him unnerved.

"What's poppin, my G?" Santana asked. Hood nodded toward the kitchen. Santana got off the couch and followed Hood into the other room.

"What's poppin, Ock, you a'ight? You enjoying yourself?" Hood asked as he sat on the countertop.

"Yeah, I'm straight, son, it's better than just being cooped up in the house," he replied.

"That's what's good. My young bull Piru think you're ready to join the fold. How you feel about that?"

"I never really asked son about it, but I hinted a couple of times to what I may want to do when the time was right. It ain't a matter if I'm ready for the fam. Question, is the fam ready for me?" Santana replied, meaning every word. He just hoped Hood didn't catch the threat he shot.

"What can you bring to the table then, lor homie?" Hood asked.

"Loyalty, honor, respect, I keep it hundred, my G. This shit been in my heart since a youngin. I'm ready when y'all ready." Santana really did have love for the movement, but it was a double-edged sword at the moment. Hood looked at him. He acted like he was convinced and Santana noticed.

"You willing to kill for niggas, ock, if need be?" Hood looked into Santana's eyes after he asked the question.

"All eleven rounds," he replied, as he tapped his hip where his Glock rested daily. Hood laughed. He'd seen so many niggas that acted tough fold, so it was a joke to him.

"We gone see," Hood replied.

***

Simfany had finished shopping; she still didn't want to head home just yet. But she had nothing else in mind to do. *Maybe I could kidnap Paris and have a girls' night out,* she thought. That sounded like a good idea. She opened the back door and put the shopping bags in the back seat. She opened the driver door and hopped in. Simfany backed out of the parking spot, making sure not to hit any parked or oncoming cars. As she pulled out into the traffic, she noticed in her rear view mirror a maroon Crown Vic with tinted windows trying to get past her. She opened her window and signalled the driver to pass. The Crown Vic drove past her and exited the mall parking lot. Simfany followed suite and hit I 95 on her way home.

Simfany arrived home an hour later to find Paris alone by herself. She carried the bags upstairs to her room. It was bad enough Paris was there every day but being left in her home alone disturbed her. *Santana should know better than that,* she thought as she shook her head in disappointment. After she dropped the bags off, Simfany came back downstairs and greeted Paris.

"What's up, Paris?" Simfany asked.

"Nothing, waiting on ya son to come back, "Paris answered.

"Where did he go?" Simfany sat down in the love seat.

"He went with Piru somewhere." Paris shrugged, basically saying she didn't know.

"What's up? You trying to go out with me tonight?" Simfany asked, looking over at Paris.

"Hell yeah!" Paris sat up excitedly.

"Get dressed and be ready. I'll be back in a second." Simfany ran upstairs and changed into a cute *Velour* sweat suit.

"You ready yet?" she called from upstairs.

"Yeah," Paris called back, standing at the bottom of the steps. Simfany came downstairs to a very beautiful awaiting Paris. The freckles that were sprayed amongst her face made her even more beautiful.

"You trying to go to the putt-putt out in Abingdon?" It was a new arcade place, equipped with laser tag and putt-putt golf. She had never been there, but she was definitely trying to see what all the hype was. Plus, if it was corny, the movie theater was right across the streets; it was Simfany's plan B.

"Yeah, I'm down."

The girls made the trip and enjoyed the night out. They even caught a new movie playing in the movie theater. On the drive home, Paris pointed out to Simfany how a maroon car was driving too close to her bumper. Simfany sped up. The car didn't follow, but the car—she had to admit—looked familiar. She just couldn't remember where she saw it before. She put it out her head as she drove the rest of the way home, jamming Cam'ron *"Come Home With Me"*.

Jamel Mitchell

Chapter Eleven

Santana sat quietly in the back of the dark sedan. The thoughts he spawned at himself were unassuming and deadly. He didn't know what he was thinking when he agreed to kill for the gang. It was true he had a lot of love for the five but killing somebody that meant no harm to him was crazy. He pushed the thought out of his head. *At the end of the day it was for the love and revenge of my mom, right?* he questioned himself. He had to deal with himself. He wasn't sure anymore.

He sat up and looked out of the window awaiting his next order. He knew nothing about the target, and the complex—or where he was at—was unfamiliar. He relied solely on Hood Ru to get him back home. Santana opened his phone to generate some light, the gun that rested on his lap was provided by TTP. He popped the clip halfway out to make sure the gun was loaded and ready to fire. The magazine indicated that the gun was halfway full. It was okay, because if

shit got real he was strapped with his own gun. Santana nervously moved around inside the car. He was getting impatient; he wanted to get it over with. Even though the car was damn near pitch-black, he felt all eyes on him. He looked up and caught Piru looking at him in the rear-view mirror. His eyes spoke volumes. He had the *'don't-let-me-down'* look on his face. Santana nodded, letting him know he understood.

"You sure you ready to do this, ock, not everybody got the heart for it. Let me know because after this, ain't no looking back!" Hood explained as he looked back at Santana from the passenger seat.

"I'm good, my G, just anxious. This gone be a first but fuck it. I'm rocking." He replied nervously. He wished it was a test in pride and saw the heart he had and called it off. But it looked like in this situation that wasn't the case. They wanted somebody dead, so he agreed to oblige. He would kill the world to get revenge for Simfany.

"Ock, here the nigga come." Hood pointed at the car slowly coming up the block.

Santana looked, eyeing the head lights creeping up O Court in Harford Square. He sighed then asked:

"So, after the nigga get out the car—rock him, then what?"

"Run back to the car and we gone. Nothing more, nothing less, but don't let the nigga get out. Hit him where he at."

"Say no more," he replied. Santana pushed aside all the fear within him and opened the door. He crept out and rushed the shadows of the parked cars closest to him. He looked back at the car that held the TTP members in it. He couldn't see them, but he was sure all eyes were still on him. He turned back around, rising from his crouching position, and looked through the parked car window. The car was looking for a parking spot. Santana crept along the side of the oval driveway, gaining yard by yard, trying to get closer without being seen.

The car parallel-parked. Santana waited patiently, inching closer and closer. The car's engine shut off. He ran along the lines of cars until he was at the driver side door. Without hesitation Santana raised the gun two feet away from the window and fired. *Boc!* The first shot shattered the window. Blood squirted from the victim's face. The body slumped into the divider.

Santana reached his arm into the car and fired. *Boc! Boc! Boc! Boc!*—he continued until the gun's barrel shot back, indicating he was out of bullets. He looked down at the body; the movement was minimum. What brought Santana out of his trance was the barking of a dog in the distance. He turned and ran, hopping in the car with his awaiting new family. After Piru dropped Santana off, he opened the door to a laughing Simfany. It was late. Paris was long gone. Not very excited, he ran upstairs closing out the world with the slamming of his door. He was perplexed.

He had just killed somebody for no reason. When he was with Piru and Hood, he showed no signs of remorse. He didn't want them to think he was weak. But in all truth he felt like crying, not because of the body he caught, but because he was dumb enough to be persuaded into doing the dumb shit. He sat and cursed himself for the bad decision making on his part. He stopped eating at himself because he knew it was a bigger picture. He laid down on his bed and fought his demons.

Santana's door opened to his room. He looked up knowing it was no one other than his mother. She stood at the door and just looked in on him. She could sense something was wrong, but said nothing at first. She wanted him to feel comfortable to talk about whatever.

"So, what's up, Tana? Why you running around slamming doors?" she asked as she sat on the corner of his dresser.

"Nothing. I'm good, ma. Just upset over some dumb shit with Paris."

"So that's what we're doing now? You lying to me. Before you keep your lie going, I'm gone let you know Paris left ten minutes before you showed up. We had been together all night. So, stop lying and tell me what the fuck is wrong!" Simfany said angrily. Santana looked down at his feet. She fished.

"Does it involve the police?" she asked calmly. He didn't have to answer; his silence was enough. "SANTANA, WHAT THE FUCK DID YOU DO?" she yelled, tired of playing his silent games.

"You don't have to yell at me, Ma." He sat and played with his hair.

"Then stop playing fucking games with me and tell me what you did?"

"I killed a nigga in Harford Square tonight," he whispered. Simfany lost her mind.

"What the fuck for, Santana? Santana why? I just got you back!" she cried. She could see the vision already; her son would be locked up for the rest of his life.

"For you," he said flatly.

"Who was it?" she asked curiously.

"I don't know." That puzzled her.

"What you mean—" She stopped mid-sentence. None of it mattered. She wiped her tears away. It was like her heart suddenly hardened. The killer instinct in her kicked in.

"You sure you killed this nigga?" she asked. He shrugged. He wasn't completely hundred percent sure, but he doubted that the nigga survived.

"When did you do this? I watched the news at eleven. I didn't hear shit 'bout nobody getting shot or killed." She remembered watching the news, and somebody being killed in Edgewood was not one of the stories.

"About eight, I don't know." Simfany grabbed hold of him.

"You look shaken. You okay?"

"Yeah, the only thing fucking with me is I didn't know son I popped."

"So why did you do it?" She was confused.

"To become Tree Top Piru," he disclosed. The anger showed in Simfany's eyes. Before she could say anything he continued. "You know why I joined those niggas. If any of them shot you I will find out. I'm gone be around them niggas for a while. You said you re-member what the nigga looked like, right? So as soon as you tell me who it may be, I'm gone body the nigga then we can go back home or wherever you wanna go. But until then fuck everybody else. It is what it is." Simfany knew she couldn't talk him out of his thirst for blood, but she could ride with him and make sure he himself would be safe.

"Just be careful and don't have none of them niggas in my house if I'm not here," she said as she rose and smacked him in his head.

"I got you."

"I love you, Santana. Never forget that."

"I love you too, pretty lady, that's why I go as hard as I do for you. I'll go to the end of the world to make your future safe, because with the connects these niggas got any day can be *our* last." She caught the part he emphasized. She knew he would do his best to protect her, and he knew it was vice versa. They were all each other had. They embraced. The doubt he had in his head for the murder he committed earlier that night vanished. Subconsciously, he didn't know, but pulling the trigger earlier was like a bitch, a high he would chase for many years to come.

***

Hood was impressed; he couldn't lie about that. The little nigga had handled his business. Now that only gave Hood more of a reason to watch him. He was probably just paranoid but he didn't believe in coincidences. Everything happened for a reason. He just didn't know if Santana was a gift or a curse. Either way he would play him closely. He felt someone tap him.

"What's up, ock?" Hood turned toward Stacks.

"Nigga, you over here daydreaming and shit." Stacks laughed. "How the lor nigga handle his? You think he ready if we need him?" Stacks asked.

"To be honest, Ru, lor nigga rock out. Nigga, if you would have seen how the nigga crept Nelo, you might have pulled your own gun. Ock, the nigga walked smoothly up to the nigga, blasted the first shot, watched him, then put his hand in the car and emptied the rest of the clip. We got another Piru on our hands. And it doesn't help these niggas chill together every walking minute." Stacks smug grin turned into a smile.

"That's what's up. But how you feel about shorty, for real?" Stacks asked. Hood understood what was asked without any explanation.

"As long as the shit with his mom don't come to fruit, I can fuck with the young bull. But you know if he shows any sign of betrayal or recognition, he becomes a plate. Shit, what do you think?" Hood waited for his response; it probably would be some bullshit ass explanation. Stacks always had some bullshit with him.

"I mean lor yo sound like he for the cause. You're worried about all the wrong shit, Ru. Don't anybody in this world know I rocked his mother but *you!*" Stacks emphasized but continued. "So, it ain't no reason to lay the young nigga sideways. It sounds like his loyalty runs deep, then ours will too. We getting too much money to put a nigga on our team we can't trust. So that larceny you got tucked in your heart, let it go. If you think at any time he may catch on, kill 'em. But until when he do, let the nigga ride like he ya own blood."

"I'm saying if that's what you want, it's done. I got love for the young bull anyway—I'm just being precautious," Hood replied.

"So, when you gone let the lor nigga know them was blanks he shot into Nelo's car?" Stacks laughed.

"You always on that bullshit, shorty. Nelo shook too. The nigga won't stop calling my phone. All of a sudden, he got the lor bread he owes me. That nigga pussy. He saw his life flash in front of his eyes literally." They both laughed.

"Whenever he ask about the kill, I'll let him know. If I think I know who he is, lor homie will ask for the satisfaction. The crazy thing is, that bitch ass nigga Nelo really got hurt. The glass from the first blast cut his face up." They shook their heads at Nelo's luck. The door opened and in came in four from the hood. Hood Ru and Stacks let the conversation die. No matter what Stacks said, Hood was going to watch Santana for his own purposes; he truly believed that his life depended on it.

Chapter Twelve

The evening news had just gone off. For the third day in a row nothing came up about the body in Harford Square. It confused Santana each time he watched the news. *Maybe I didn't hit the nigga with every shot. Bullshit, that first shot would have killed him anyway,* he told himself.

He just didn't understand. He knew them TTP niggas was gone be mad, but it was nothing he could do about it. The dude survived by God's hand, not his. Worse come to worse, when the nigga got out of the hospital, he'd run down on him again. The thoughts that ran through his head were getting more and more menacing as the days passed.

As he sat and pondered, the smell of smoke caught his attention. He got off the couch and walked into a smoke-filled kitchen. Paris had the screen door open, waving the smoke out as best as she could. It really wasn't helping much. "Damn, ma, you trying burn us out of house and home?" Santana asked teasingly. The facial expression was that of disappointment. She frowned. Santana walked up to her and gently kissed her on the neck to let her know it was okay. He looked at the stove, looked at Paris and burst out laughing.

"Nigga, what's so funny?" She got angry and began to turn red from embarrassment.

"Ma, when you got something burning, you got to make sure you turn the stove off first or—" He laughed again. "Or the shit gone continue to burn." He reached past her to cut the stove off. Santana opened the patio door all the way, leaving the screen in its place. He turned and faced Paris.

"It's okay, baby. I'm gone go to the shell and get some chicken wings. What were you making anyway?" He looked at the pot; all that was left was just a dark piece of meat.

"Steak," she answered, lips poked out. Santana kissed her; he didn't want to hurt her feelings. He grabbed her into a close embrace and talked to her.

"I love everything about you, ma, can't lie. Ain't felt this way since I was back home. You bring the good out of me. So, don't let this spoil your evening. Please. I'm about to go get these chicken wings. You want anything? He kissed her neck again, forcing her to moan.

"I can't think with you kissing all over me." She smiled.

"My bad," he apologized.

"Just get me some junk food, I guess. You gone cook for me when you get back, right?" She gave him the sad puppy dog eyes.

"That shit doesn't work on me. I invented those eyes. But I got you. It's late as fuck. You staying over here tonight?" he asked seriously.

"Yeah, my mother ain't gone trip. She probably not home either. Just hurry up back and stay out of that path. Take the long way. Niggas be acting up out here at night." "A'ight, I got you, ma." He let her go, grabbed his hoodie off the chair and left out the patio door. As he stepped off the patio into the backyard, he told her: "Leave this door open. I don't have my keys on me. My mom should be back any minute." "Got you," she replied. Santana walked around to the opening near the dumpsters. That ended the row of town houses that he lived on. A set of eight houses started on the other side of him. He walked past the parked cars, making his way to the main road. He looked down the street to make sure no cars were coming. He did the same as he looked up the hill. The light illuminated off the ground, indicating one was on its way. That gave Santana time to jog across the street.

As he stepped foot on the sidewalk, a car came flying down the hill past him. Santana looked at the car as it drove by. He had to admit the car was nice. The burgundy exterior and tinted windows made the car stand out. It kind of reminded him of a police car, though. That was the only thing he didn't like about it.

He walked through the short cut to get to the gas station. The story that people told was for real, he thought as he walked into the pitch-black area. Instinctively, he reached for his gun. He pulled his hoodie up and tucked it behind the handle of his Glock 26. Nervously, he walked. He wanted to turn around but said *fuck it* and continued on his way to the store. The same car that drove past with the tinted windows stopped in the middle of the street, at the top of the hill. The driver got out and came to the leafless trees, peering down into the darkness. He was looking for something. Santana stopped moving. He didn't want the driver to know he was still on the path.

"Santana!" the driver called out. That made Santana nervous. He didn't answer. He couldn't tell who it was, so it was no way he was going to reply.

"Santana!" the driver called yet again. Santana stood still. The driver turned to leave. The sound of his phone made him jump almost out of his skin. He looked down at his pocket. The phone was lite up his pocket as it rung. In the dark the phone lit up the night. He pulled it as fast as he could to stop the flashing. The driver turned back around. Santana was sure he noticed the bright ass light coming from his pants pocket.

"Santana!" he called out again.

"Yo!" Santana answered, cursing himself afterwards. "Who is that?" Santana asked, looking at the top of the hill.

"It's Hood, ock!" the driver yelled back. The driver's reply made Santana take his gun off his hip. He knew that wasn't Hood Ru on the top of the hill. But he played along anyway.

"Oh, what's up, Ru?"

"It's Hood, ock, not Ru." The driver moved closer to the path. Santana could only see one arm as he looked up at him. His phone lit up again as his ring tone vibrated in his pocket. The driver pulled his other arm from behind his back. Santana was too busy trying to get his phone to shut off, he didn't see dude raise his gun. *Boc!* The crack in the air made Santana get low. Without looking he fired back, running deeper into the darkness. *Boc! Boc! Boc!* Each shot was only inches away from him. It was obvious that the shooter couldn't see him; he was just shooting. Santana tried to run forward, *Boc!* Another shot rang out, stopping him in his tracks. *Fuck this shit,* he thought to himself. He up'd his strap and aimed at the dark figure at the top of the hill. The shooter let another round of shots go and ran around to the driver side. The shooter hopped in the car and peeled off.

Santana wasn't taking any chances; he ran full speed to the Shell station, gun in hand. He refused to die in Maryland. As the car peaked the top of the hill to leave Meadowood, Santana fired. *Boc!* *Boc!* The bullets sent sparks off the car. The Maroon Crown Victoria made a right, exiting Meadowood. The car slowed as it drove past the gas station and beeped his horn. Santana raised his gun again to fire, but the car sped off. He peaked around the comer into the store; the clerk was on the phone. He took no chance to stick around. He ran up the stairs into Meadowood. Santana got to his patio safely. He went to pull the patio door and it was locked. "Man, what the fuck! I told this bitch to leave the fucking door open," he said out loud, cursing Paris. He tried the door again, knowing the outcome. Gun in hand, he ran around the section of townhouses to the front. As he hit the Corner, he saw his mother's Tahoe sitting in their parking spot. He looked both ways as he came out from in between the row homes. He gripped his Glock tighter and ran to the front door. He banged hard. A couple seconds later he heard the locks being turned. "Hurry the fuck up!" he yelled, still looking at the street for any oncoming cars. His heart was racing at 100 miles per hour. The door finally opened; he ran in. Santana stumbled into the living room as Tijuana opened the door.

"Hey, baby bo—" Her words were cut short by the gun in Santana's hand.

"Simfany!" Tijuana screamed. He didn't look hurt, but he knew she was scared by the gun alone.

"Oh my God! Baby, are you okay?" Tijuana asked.

"Yeah, I'm hundred. Where my mom at?" He kicked his shoes off and ran into the kitchen, turning all lights off.

"Simfany!" Tijuana called out again.

"What's up, damn you yelling and shit. What?" Simfany asked with an attitude as she came to the top of the steps.

"Santana's down here looking all crazy with a gun in his hand." Before Tijuana could finish her sentence, Simfany was running down the steps. The sight she saw brought fire to her eyes.

"Baby?" she called out. He looked up as she approached.

"Talk to me, what happened?" she asked as she eased the gun out of his hand.

"Somebody just tried to end my career," he replied.

"English, Santana, I don't know what the fuck you're talking about," Simfany stated.

"Some nigga tried to kill me in the path behind the Shell." He looked up. She could see the fear mixed with rage in his eyes.

"Paris always tells you to stay the fuck out of that alley, Santana. What does the nigga look like?" she asked intently.

"I don't know. He started busting at the top of the hill. If I didn't take the path, you'd be out there claiming my body. Son drove like a burgundy looking cop car. The bubble ones." It was the only way he could explain the car.

"A Crown Vic," Tijuana spoke up.

"Yeah. I think."

Something clicked in Simfany's head about the car.

"You said burgundy or was it maroon?"

"What the fuck is maroon?" he asked.

"It's like a deep blood red." She didn't know how to explain the color, so she tried her best.

"Yeah, kind of, it was dark out there. The nigga had tinted windows. The shit was clean. That's what made me take notice in the first place."

Paris came halfway down the stairs and took a seat. She looked through the bars at him. She was worried, he realized. They locked eyes until she broke the gaze. Santana over looked the gesture.

"A maroon Vic been popping up a lot of places I been as of recently," Simfany said out loud. She meant to keep it to herself. *Fuck,* she thought as Santana looked up at her.

"What you mean?"

"The night me and Paris went to the putt-putt and a movie, the same car was damn near driving bumper to bumper. I sped up, but he didn't follow so I thought nothing more about it. I saw the car somewhere else before, I just can't think where. I'm thinking at White Marsh. I'm not sure though." What Simfany had just told them made Santana's blood boil. To know that somebody had been following his mother made him sick. What was killing him the most was nobody knew who the person was. *Oh shit,* he thought suddenly. He reached into his pants pocket and grabbed out his phone.

He turned it on. The screen lit up it showed two missed calls, both from Paris. Strange, but he said nothing to nobody about it. He searched through his phone until he came upon the number he was looking for.

He called the number. The person on the other end of the phone answered within seconds of the call.

"What's poppin', blood?" Piru asked on the other end of the phone.

"My G, Hood with you?" he asked.

"Yeah, they just let him and G ride in the club. Hold up. Hold up." He heard the other voices in the background talking.

"A'ight—Yo, Tana. My bad, the bouncer had to check this fake ass ID so I can get in the club." The music in the background became extremely loud.

"I'm looking for the nigga right now. Excuse me—There he go." All he could hear was a scuffle kind of sound coming from the other end.

"What's poppin', bull!" Hood yelled into the phone; he tried to talk over the music.

"What club y'all niggas at? It's loud as shit." Santana fished.

"We at the Docks, college night. It's jumping too, my nigga. All type of broads from Coppin in this bitch." Hood sounded hyped.

"Have fun, my G, just holla at me when you get back."

"A'ight, ock, Westside." The line went dead. The call eased his mind. It was no way Hood could have made it to the city that fast. Tijuana and Simfany looked at each other then looked back at him. They didn't get the point of the phone call.

"I'll explain—Give me a second," he told both Tijuana and his mother. He got up from the couch and walked to the railing of the stairs. Paris had her head tucked in between her knees.

"Ma." Santana hit her leg. She looked up, her eyes were watery and bloodshot.

"Yeah," Paris answered.

"I gotta holla at my family tonight. A nigga tried to kill me out there. There's a lot that has to be discussed and I can only say it around people I trust with my life. Before you start to show ya ass,

I'm not saying I don't trust you. But a lot will be said tonight and I don't want to take the chance of it being repeated." She poked her lip out and nodded.

"I understand. Now you don't trust me? That's crazy, but it's okay. I'm going home. I'll holla at you." Paris sounded angry. She stood up and walked the rest of the way downstairs.

"So that's how you acting?" Santana asked smugly.

"How am I acting, nigga? You asked me to go home, not the other way around."

"You got it, ma. I don't want to argue with you, Paris. Please just give me until tomorrow. Can you do that? Please."

"Yeah, my bad. I'm trippin'. I just want to spend time with you." Her voice lightened back up. He opened his arms for her to come forward. She did, and they embraced.

"Damn, she ain't even give you none yet and you whipped." Simfany made light of the situation. Everybody but Santana burst out laughing. He turned around and glared at his mother. She mouthed: *My bad.*

"That's what you think." He turned back to Paris. "Be safe and hit me when you get in the house to let me know you got home safely." He opened the door and she walked outside.

Paris turned.

"I love you, Santana, you be safe too." And she continued through the door and down the block without looking back. He closed the door. The atmosphere got serious again. He sat down next to Tijuana.

"So, what's up?" Simfany asked.

"Hold up, ma?" He looked at Tijuana. "You know this conversation ain't even for me and you, but I gotta make sure. Please don't repeat anything you hear in this house to no one. I really love you a lot and I got the upmost for you. In more ways than you know. I just need you to understand this shit may get serious. I'm not sure what gone come out of this, but if somebody dies I don't want to worry about my freedom." He was blunt to the core. After a pause, he went on. "I swear I mean no disrespect, but you can't tell what you don't know, so you can leave if you want." He made eye contact with her.

"Shit, baby boy, I'm rocking with you and my ace boon. I ain't killing shit or being around if it does go down. But I'm here now. The exact same when I needed you. Does that satisfy you?" Tijuana asked.

"Hundred." He smiled. Their look lingered for a little while too long.

"Anyways, what you talking about? What was the call to Hood about?" Simfany asked as she leaned forward with her legs tucked under her.

"The reason I called Hood was because the nigga tried to use his name to get me to come to him. Hood the nigga Byrd use to fuck with on the brick tip. I don't know, it was a long shot. I thought Hood was the top nigga, but he ain't, his man is. The nigga Stacks. I fuck with Piru the hardest. That's a real nigga. I don't think neither of them niggas knows anything about you. I haven't met the dude Stacks yet. This shit crazy. It wasn't any of them TTP niggas that clapped at me. I can't say for sure, but I think I got this one right. Them niggas had plenty of time to kill me if they wanted me dead."

"So who do you think it could be then, Santana?" Simfany got frustrated. She couldn't believe her ears. She was praying that Santana wasn't falling for the bullshit them niggas was throwing his way. Her not really knowing herself, she didn't comment on it.

"What about the nigga Jimdog?" Tijuana asked. They both shrugged.

"That's a good question. That's the only other nigga I can think of besides these TTP niggas. But mom said Carlos had son on a short leash." He looked over to his mother for an answer.

"How much do you believe of that?" he asked.

"I can call Carlos and ask," Simfany replied. She grabbed Santana's phone and dialed the number from memory. Carlos didn't answer. Simfany redialed the number. This time she got his voicemail after the second ring.

"Man, what the fuck! I don't know why Carlos is not answering his phone!" she exclaimed frustratingly.

"Ma, calm down and call from ya phone. He doesn't know my number." She sucked her teeth and got up. Her phone was all the way upstairs in her room. Santana watched as she took off up the stairs. Tijuana laughed at Simfany's laziness.

"How you been though, ma? How you been holding up? How my goon doing?" Santana tried to make small talk until his mother returned.

"Drew's fine, he walking around looking lost all day. He misses you for real. Have you been writing him?" The look on his face told her enough. "Santana, you need to sit down and write him, he's worried about you being out here solo. He asks about you every time I work King Hall. Write him, Santana. But as far as me I'm good, can be better but I'm doing okay." She finished just as Simfany was making her way down the stairs. She was in the middle of a conversation. They listened intently.

"Oh yeah? So, if I see this nigga around here again, I'm going to kill him. That nigga tried to kill my son, Carlos— Keep him in your city then or—" Simfany stopped and listened.

"No, Carlos, we good. But keep that nigga out there. I'm not playing, Carlos, if I see that car or that nigga anywhere near here, I swear on Dracula I'm going to put hundred rounds in him. I'm dead serious, you let that nigga know what I said. No, thank you—You too. You be safe also. Alright—okay, Carlos—bye." Simfany hit the end button on her cell phone and looked up menacingly.

"A'ight, let me get straight to the point. Jimdog drives a maroon Crown Vic and Carlos said he hadn't heard from him in a couple of days. I saw the nigga last week when me and Paris went out. What I do not understand is why he didn't ambush me and Paris on route 24. You know it's always dark as hell at night between the Mc Donald's exit and the exit to Hanson Road. It doesn't matter where you see that car, Santana, you already know what you have to do. Either that or get killed. I refuse to let you die. So please don't hesitate." He nodded. Tijuana sat there at awe. She'd never seen her friend in this light. *Shawty go hard*, Tijuana thought to herself. Simfany continued. "Just be cautious on who you're around. He seems to know exactly where to be. Chill in the house with Paris a couple of days to see what happens. I'm good. I'm gone set the little nigga on fire if I see him near us again." "I'm gone come with you when you leave; you leave I leave. But I'm good. He not gone come right back especially if he think we might know it was him. He's a shooter, but by no means is he stupid. Paris straight. It's something weird about her tonight though. Oh yeah, did you lock the patio door when you came in?" Santana asked. Simfany shook her head.

"I expressly told Paris to leave the door open. I didn't have my keys on me. I came back and the patio was locked. I didn't say nothing about it because I assumed you or Tijuana locked the door." Santana looked from Simfany to Tijuana

"It sounds like lover girl wants you dead, baby boy." Tijuana spoke what was on her mind.

"What makes you say that?" Simfany asked curiously, taking the words right out of Santana's mouth.

"Okay but explain what happened and why you went to the store in the first place. My brother kept the cute hoes on deck to set niggas up. The broads are creative too. It's crazy. But tell me what happened." Santana explained from the time the news was over to the time he came running home. He left out nothing. Simfany couldn't see Paris doing Santana like that even though it was possible. Regardless, she still listened to Tijuana's theory.

"This how I see it adds up. Every time y'all see Jimdog she around, besides your time at the mall, right Simfany?" Tijuana asked.

"Kind of she was here when I left for the mall but she was lying on Santana's lap sleeping."

"She wasn't sleeping, ma, I was just rubbing her scalp," Santana corrected his mother.

"Alright, let me finish," Tijuana continued. "Maybe the only reason he didn't ambush you that night was because Paris was with you. I don't know. I might be hundred percent wrong, but burning a steak? Really? Come on. Who burns a steak? Not only that but she leaves the stove on. That was a dumb bitch move. I believe she intentionally started the smoke. This is all a guess. You leave, she calls Jimdog, he speeds down hoping to catch you going into the path, or even better he hopes to catch you walking outside the path like *she* suggested. My only problem is, you watched him pass as you were hitting the cut. He made a U-turn obviously, knowing you wouldn't' t be out the cut yet. He gets out of his car, calls ya name a couple of times, you said you didn't answer, but then your phone rings, lighting up your pocket. It was basically giving your location away. Right, that's what happens so far, right?" Santana. Tijuana continued. "Your phone not only rings once, it rings twice. The second almost proved to be deadly. You finally get back and realize she was the person on ya miss call list. Of course, you think nothing of it because that's your lor girlfriend. Too much adds up against her. I don't know, Tana. I'm just saying do what you do but watch her." Tijuana finished, she explained the way she saw things and why she felt like such. It was only up to them to listen.

"You do have a lot of points, but even if she does burn the steak how would she know I would want to go to the store with a house full of food?" Santana tried to break down Tijuana's theory for his own good.

"It was a chance that I pretty sure they both were willing to play out. If you don't go to the store, no harm done, but if you decide you want to be lazy and go to the Shell station then it was murder she wrote. You just escaped with your life *this time*. I don't have the answers. I just see shade, that's all. I love you, Santana and I refuse to let some bum ass bitch do you like that, especially if I see through that fake ass smile."

Damn, he thought. It all sounded plausible, but he just couldn't see Paris playing that kind of role. But he made a mental note to watch her.

"Listen, it's late and I'm tired, but Santana, if what Tijuana says has any truth to it, those dreads will wash up in the Inner Harbor and I'm dead serious. I like the little girl, but if she played a part in trying to have you killed, whether it worked or not, I will bury her then pay for the funeral. I'm going to bed. It's going on two o'clock. Tijuana, is you staying tonight?" Simfany asked as she got up and yawned.

"Nah, I gotta work tomorrow," Tijuana replied, getting up also. She opened her arms for Simfany to show her some love. Santana watched them hug.

"Call me," Simfany said.

"I will."

"Hold up, ma, let me get my gun back."

"I'll give it to you when you come upstairs. Lock the door when T leaves. Bye, girl."

Simfany made her way up the stairs sluggishly.

"I'm out anyway. I see you soon. Please stay out of harm's way and watch your girlfriend. Okay?" Santana nodded. "I love you, baby boy."

"Love you too, ma." He opened the door for her. Tijuana stood in the doorway. Before she left, she cupped his chin and kissed him passionately, catching him off guard. He kissed her back. They fell into *unison*. Tijuana had to pull back; she was getting lost in their kiss.

"You just remember what I said," she stated as walked down the grass to her car. Tijuana held eye contact with Santana the whole time; she pulled off leaving him lost for words.

Chapter Thirteen

Despite Tijuana's speech and warning, Santana played with fire. He never said a word to Paris about Tijuana's theory. He truthfully never paid no attention it himself. The kiss told him enough. The love he had for Paris made Santana blind, and at times he knew that. What used to just be chill sessions became fuck sessions, pulling Santana in deeper and deeper, literally.

The thought about the incident with Jimdog no longer had him on edge. Of course, he stayed strapped everywhere he went; he just didn't think Jimdog would show his face again for a while. However, Santana made a promise to himself if Jimdog did show up, he would blow his head off his shoulders.

Santana sat up in his king size bed and stretched. It had been a crazy week for him, what with the body he caught in Harford Square, Jimdog trying to smoke him, and Paris. He gripped his mind around the facts. At first he was blind to the fact because the pussy was so good. But as he revaluated the past, he had no choice but to think about the inevitable. He might or might not be lying with a snake. He looked over at her beautiful, freckled face. *A beautiful snake*, he joked to himself. He couldn't read her, but he swore her heart was pure. But guessing and knowing was two different things. Unless she just blatantly showed signs of disloyalty, he wouldn't act upon Tijuana's suspicions. The kiss he shared with Tijuana also threw him for a loop because the theory about Paris could be based on jealousy. He even talked to his mother about the situation. Whether she wanted to admit it or not, it seems as if the theory was out of pure jealousy. He didn't know. He was really confused about the whole thing for real. Plus the pussy was just so good. He smiled every time he thought about their lovemaking. He felt Paris stir on the other side of the bed; he looked over and watched her. She stretched under the cover but came up when she had realized he was no longer lying down.

"Hey, sexy?" She smiled, showing off her pearly whites.

"What's up, beautiful?" he replied, bending over, kissing her on the top of her head. She covered her mouth as she yawned.

"I see you're up early again. What's the matter?" she asked. *You*, he thought.

"Just thinking about a lot of different shit. Just about life in general." He looked into her tired eyes.

"Talk to me, tell me what's on ya mind. Maybe I can help." She moved closer, resting her head on his lap. The gesture alone made Santana's man jump in excitement. Seductively, Paris reached for his piece. Only to be stopped by Santana's hand.

"Please, ma, not right now, I got too much shit on my mind," he said, his hand still clutching his dick. She attempted to move his hand.

"Well, then I know exactly what to do to invert them thoughts." She playfully fought for what she wanted. But he got angry.

"Ma, I'm good right now!" he said with a lot of bass in his voice. It just seemed like when he was caught in deep thought she would throw the pussy at him. His mind was starting to play tricks on him. Tricks or no tricks, his life was on the line. He was going solely off of instinct. Paris looked up at him with the stink face and slid back to the side of her bed. Santana sighed. He knew he was wrong for spazzing on her like that.

"Ma, look my bad, I'm just—"

"Nah, Santana, you good. No need to explain for real. I understand. I overstepped my boundaries. Shit, you got it." She got out the bed angry, walking away in her *Victoria's Secret* underwear. The red lace matched perfectly with her glowing caramel complexion. Paris slamming the bathroom brought Santana out of his seductive trance. He knew she was pissed, but he didn't really care. He got out the bed from under the white sheets, wearing only a pair of boxers. The dresser that stood directly in front of his bed held a 27'-inch flat screen TV; the channel was on ESPN, muted. He watched the segment for a second; the analyst was talking about the new entries to the league, LeBron James, Carmelo Anthony and Dwayne Wade. All the hype was surrounded by the high school standout LeBron James, but by far his favorite player was Carmelo. He was a diehard Syracuse fan. After the segment went off, Santana opened the top drawer in search for a tee shirt and shorts. He pulled out a shirt and put it on. But something caught his eye as strange. His mother kept guns strategically stashed with in every room and he knew those spots, but the Glock 26 that laid in the drawer confused him. He left the dresser draw open and climbed back on to his bed and moved his pillow from the far side of his bed. His gun was gone. He instantly got furious. He climbed off the bed and continued to get dressed. After his shorts were on, he picked the gun out of the drawer and checked the clip. The clip was still full, but the bullet in the chamber wasn't there. He grew angrier until he remembered he never put a bullet in the chamber at night just in case the trigger was pulled he would still be safe. The point he was stressing: the gun was in the drawer and not under the pillow where he remembers putting it. Paris came back into the room stomping around still with an attitude. Santana tucked the gun in his waist band and turned to confront Paris.

"Why you move my gun?" he asked angrily. *She wants a muthafuckin argument, she got it,* he thought as he looked at her, waiting for an answer. She was dressed now. She ignored him.

"Hello, Paris. Why the fuck did you move my gun!" he yelled. He was getting annoyed. That caught her attention.

"Nigga, who the fuck you yelling at?" she stepped forward. He laughed.

"Shit, you got it. Stop stomping around this bitch, my mom's still asleep." He moved closer, so he wouldn't be so loud and continued. "Why did you move my gun?"

"Because don't nobody wants to be asleep with a gun facing their head, but you, Santana. That's why." She replied with a deceptive flaying stare.

"My nigga, if you wasn't snooping through my shit you wouldn't know what's under *my* pillows."

"Nigga, fuck you. I'm ya bitch. I got access to anything in this room. Do I not?" she said as she twisted her head to the side.

"Nah, Paris, you don't. This is *my* domain. Stay away from the shit that's gone save my life. Because trust and believe you not stopping any bullets if they swung my way." His last comment hurt Paris; her eyes began to water.

"Damn, baby, that's how you feel?" So, what are we doing, Santana? Having fun? Because I need to know what it is."

"Just don't touch my guns, everything else I don't care about. Stay away from this." He pulled his shirt up, showing her the black steel of the Glock. He continued. "These ten shots that this shit hold in the clip keep me breathing a day longer, my nigga."

"Don't call me that."

"What?"

"Ya nigga. That's not us. So, please, Santana, stop."

"Anyway, *Paris,* all I ask is don't play with my life." He turned and sat down at the end of his bed and unmuted the TV. The sports analysts were still debating about the trio. He listened intently to them talk until suddenly it was no more picture or sound. The TV was turned off. Santana turned as Paris was putting the remote on the nightstand.

"What's up, Paris?" He looked back at her.

"Nigga, what type of shit you on this morning? You want me to leave?"

"That's ya choice," he said simply. Paris nodded.

"You got it, Santana." Her eyes watered. She sucked her bottom lip in between her teeth. She was angry. He took a deep breath. He was being an asshole and he knew it, but his pride wouldn't let him stop.

"So, what's up? You turned the TV off for a reason?" he asked, looking at her unflinchingly.

"Why are you acting like this towards me? I didn't do shit to you, Santana. I'm sorry I moved your stupid ass gun. But still don't treat me like I'm the fucking enemy." She continued, but Santana didn't pay attention to the following words after her last comment. *She right, she ain't the enemy. What would make her say that?* His thought process was all fucked up. He was overthinking her words. *Fuck it,* he thought.

"What makes you say that?" He turned fully around towards her.

"What? About the sex?" she asked confusingly, obviously still hurt and mad.

"Nah, about you being the enemy. What made you say that?"

"I don't know, that's just how you make me feel sometimes, especially when Tijuana's over here. I can't keep fighting you, Santana." That took him aback; he was confused as fuck. And the look on her face gave it away; she knew she fucked up. He played dumb.

"Oh yeah, Paris. Fuck you talking about? This the first time we ever had an argument since we been together. Fuck all that. Just explain to me how you feel like the enemy." Paris being smart let her last comment go, hoping he wouldn't read in between the lines. She responded fast, trying to get out of her last jam, only digging a deeper grave.

"Ever since the night the dude in the maroon Vic tried to shoot you near the Shell, you been acting funny. You made me leave that night, remember, because you said you didn't trust me. But you let Tijuana stay. That hurt. And now you talking 'bout that gun is the only thing that will protect you. How that's supposed to make—"

"Hold up, how you know 'bout the maroon Vic?" he asked suspiciously.

"Nigga, I heard you tell Hood over the phone the other day." Santana thought for a minute. He told Hood about the car, but nobody knew about the color and make of the car besides him, his mother and Tijuana. She had him thinking bad thoughts. She realized the look all too well.

"Are you serious? Nigga, this what the fuck I mean, stupid ass nigga. I was with Simfany the night *I* noticed the fucking car. You ran in the house that night, remember, I came down and sat on the steps while you ran to that Tijuana bitch. Remember, Santana! Huh, do you? And I'm the fucking enemy, right! That's what the fuck you wanna hear, nigga, you wanna hear that I had something to do with all the bullshit that been happening so you can have explanations for your paranoid ass thoughts!" She was fuming. She got louder as her anger rose.

"You don't remember when you said the car was burgundy, a dark blood red. And that little bitch of yours corrected you and said maroon. No. No, excuse me, I apologize. Simfany was who corrected you. Then you described it to be a fucking police car! She grabbed her pocketbook, shoes and coat out of the closet. Santana sat on the bed and felt stupid.

"My bad ma. I'm just—"

"No need to explain shit to me, Santana. I got the message." The door to his room opened. Simfany stood in the door frame, wiping the sleep out of her eyes.

"What the fuck y'all so loud for, Paris?" Simfany asked looking a mess.

"Your son thinks I want to have him killed," Paris replied. Simfany looked over at Santana and shook her head. She sighed.

"Why do you say that Paris? Calm down. You might have misunderstood—" Paris cut Simfany off.

"Excuse me, Ms. Vasquez," Paris said as she attempted to get out the door. Simfany looked Paris in her eyes; she saw that Paris was serious. She moved to the side to let Paris go.

"Thank you." Paris stepped out into the hallway to leave but stopped. She needed to say something before she left. She walked back into the room, tears streaming down her face.

"I loved you, Santana. I'm in love with you, Santana. But this right here I can't do. I can't handle this kind of emotional strain. I wanted to be the mother of your children. But I would never be able to replace the thought of you thinking I would want you dead."

"I didn't—"

"I know you didn't say it, but I know what you meant. The look you gave me was enough. That shit *killed* me inside. If you thought this whole time, I was the enemy, why would you continue to fuck me, go to sleep with me, leave your gun around me? You know why because you know I'm not your fucking enemy. And deep in that head of yours you know that. Santana, you are your own enemy." Paris wiped her face, hugged Simfany and walked out the door.

Santana sat at the end of the bed lost for words. He fucked up and he knew it. He watched Simfany look down at Paris as she made her way down the steps. Paris got dressed, ready to embrace the cold weather. She shook her head and wiped her face.

"Go get her, Santana. You broke that girl's heart. I told you not to listen to Tijuana's little theory. That's all it was, Santana, a theory to figure what was going on. A lot of things add up and some shit amount to nothing. You might have just lost the best thing that could have happened to you out here. Go get her." Hearing the words coming out of his mother's mouth, he knew he was wrong. It was just the paranoia he had lately that made him question everybody's loyalty. He had a lot of love for Paris, enough to warrant an explanation from her. He put his Nike boots on and ran down the steps in hopes of catching Paris.

As he opened the door, the cold air blew hard against the thin fabric of his t-shirt. *Fuck! It's cold out this muthafucka.* He looked to the right and saw Paris walking across the street.

"Paris!" he yelled, trying to get her attention.

"Paris!" he called again. She looked both ways before she crossed the street. He cursed himself and took off after her. As he caught up to her, he yelled her name again. This time she turned around to the sound of his voice. Paris had dried tear streaks running along her chin.

"What, Santana? Your intentions were made clear. I'm gone. No need to chase me. I will always love you, Santana, but I swear I can't do this. I'm sorry." He walked closer to her and cupped her face. He looked her deep into her eyes.

"I'm sorry, ma," he stated as he leaned in and kissed her wet lips. Paris moved her face to the left to get out of his hold.

"I can't do this. I can't be with someone that thinks I would knowingly kill them. I'm sorry. Now please let me go. Take care of yourself."

"Ma, please." He grabbed her arm. Paris wiped away the fresh tears that began to fall from her eyes. She tried to speak but got choked up.

"I'm sorry," she mouthed as she pulled away from his grip and continued through the path. He sighed. *Fuck.* The cold air had him shivering in seconds, reminding him to get back inside before he froze to death. He stayed planted and watched Paris walk up the path until she was no longer in sight. He turned around and ran back home. Simfany was seated in the living room when Santana came back into the house. She searched his face for any sign of worry.

"You okay?" she asked him.

With his hand resting on the banister, he replied: "Yeah, I fucked up. Ain't shit I can do about it now. She moved my gun from under my pillow and what Tijuana had said made me start feeling some type way. Even after she left, I still feel that she's hiding something. It might not be as big, or it may not hurt me but the aura I get at times from her ain't hundred all the time. Plus, I wasn't feeling the whole situation with my gun at the time. At the end of the day, she's right, I don't trust her. Never really did. I don't trust anybody but you. I was slipping anyway. It should never have gone that far in the first place."

"You'll be okay. You like the girl. It's natural for you to feel how you do. But you're talking reckless for no reason. You don't have to convince me. You gotta be real with yourself. Enough about her. You want something to eat before I leave?" She rose from the couch.

"No, and where are you going so early?"

"Baltimore—to the mall," she lied.

"What mall?"

"Damn nosey, Mondawmin Mall, dad," she said sarcastically. He laughed.

"Buy me some Uptowns while you're there, please. Nah, as a matter of a fact, can you get me the new Barkley's that just came out. They go with that Nets jersey you bought me. Thank you, pretty lady." He hugged his mother and went upstairs.

"I ain't getting your bad ass shit," she said, knowing she would. Instead of going into the kitchen like she thought about, she walked upstairs and got dressed. She put on a simple outfit, sweatpants, a white t-shirt, and a pair of Timbs. She opened Santana's door to check on him before she left. He was so engrossed in ESPN he didn't hear the door open.

"I'm out, Tana," she told him.

"Love you, pretty lady," he said without turning around.

"Love you too, baby," she replied as she closed his door. Simfany went back into her room and grabbed her purse, looked into her vanity mirror and left. Simfany's drive to Baltimore had nothing to do with shopping. Her plan was to search for Jimdog. She knew she couldn't ride through Baltimore in her Tahoe. She needed a rental. There was a rental car place on route 40 she found awhile back called *Enterprise;* it was right across the street from the McDonald's that rested on Pulaski. She rented a 2003 black Dodge Durango.

After she parked her Tahoe on the lot, she pulled out of the parking, going down Pulaski highway.

Simfany made it into Baltimore 45 minutes later. She pulled up to the mall to buy Santana's shoes. She ran to the Downtown Locker Room and bought the Barkley's he wanted.

After she made her way back to the rental, the only other stop she would make would be to confront Jimdog to end the bullshit once and for all. Simfany pulled out of Mondawmin and headed to East Baltimore.

Chapter Fourteen

"Where the lor goon everybody keeps talking about?" Stacks asked Piru.

"Shit, I don't know. Ever since that shit with Nelo, blood been falling back. I can go scoop the lor nigga if you want." Piru replied as he jarred up the weed that laid in front of him.

"Why the lor nigga don't be out there getting money with y'all? What, he not hungry?"

Piru shrugged. *Nigga, I don't know,* he thought to himself. "Santana stay fresh, so I assume he straight," Piru answered.

"Give lor yo some work on the house, just to see what he can do with it." Hood and Tez-mo walked in the door, pulling the cold air in with them. Both men walked through and showed their respectful love. Hood sat down in the chair next to Piru.

"What's poppin', Ock? Fuck you nut ass niggas doing?"

"Fuck it look like, nigga?" Piru looked up.

"Nigga, fuck you," Hood said flatly. Hood pulled a Dutch out his pocket and split it through the middle to empty out the guts. Stacks watched Hood skillfully roll the Dutch Master.

"Ru, what you think about putting the lor nigga Santana on the block?" Stacks asked.

"What you mean? Give the young bull a pack?" Hood was confused.

"Yeah."

"Why would we put him on the block? If he trying to get money, I got him, but my niggas sell they own work, ock!" Hood said, looking up from the blunt.

"You know what I meant. He didn't ask?" Stacks reclined in the sofa in the living room.

Hood gave Stacks a smug look. He hated when Stacks played that top shot card, especially when it came to the 'get money' side of things. Hood built the empire they stood on. Stacks knew his best friend's look all too well and let the subject go. On to the next one.

"Did anybody holla at youngin about Nelo?" Stacks changed the subject.

"Nah, I talked to the nigga a couple of days ago. He was supposed to hit me back, but never did. He good, the lor nigga a'ight. He—" Hood choked on the smoke he had just inhaled. He continued to cough. "The lor nigga a G," Hood continued through bloodshot eyes.

"Damn, you gone smoke all my weed and not pass the blunt? Nigga, you tripping." Piru looked at Hood across the table.

"My bad, ock, that shit some fire though. No wonder you doing numbers out there. That shit belong in a jar." He coughed some more as he passed the Dutch.

"Tez-mo, how much you make off that package Kevin gave you?" Piro asked, blunt in hand.

"Like five thousand six hundred dollars. That's after I paid him back for the front. Why? What's up, shorty?"

"Just wanted to see what Essex was hitting for. Kev told me you do your thing out there, that's why I asked," Piru stated.

"Oh yeah, anybody hear about the shootout in Meadowood like a week ago?"

"Yeah, why? What's up?" Hood was curious.

"Mike told me Piru's lor pup start banging on somebody. What's the lor niggas name again? Man, fuck—Oh yeah, yeah, the lor nigga Santana. Mike only told me a lor bit. He said the lor nigga came out the dark letting that thing bark at some car that was speeding off," Tez-mo explained. Stacks sat up.

"Yo, Piru go get shorty and make sure he a'ight," Stacks said as if he was truly concerned about Santana. And truth be told, he was. What Hood didn't know was Stacks shot Simfany over hearsay, so he felt obligated to look after Santana. Stacks never felt remorseful about anything he has ever done before. But shooting a female over a rumor was some bullshit. He thought she had something to do with Byrd's death. He wouldn't show his cards, but he was willing to play fair.

"Stacks?" Hood tapped his foot. "Ock—Stacks— Nigga, you over there daydreaming and shit. You down, shorty? I'm gone go scoop the nigga up, you riding?" Hood grabbed the keys to his car.

"Fuck it, I'll ride with you." Stacks agreed, getting up from the couch.

"Tez, y'all niggas stay 050, ock, we be back. Have the young bull some Bailey ready. He might need it to ease his mind."

"Got you, homie," Piru said as he inhaled one last time before passing the Dutch.

"Westside," Hood and Stacks said simultaneously.

"You already know," Piru answered.

"Westside, homie," Tez-mo replied. They walked out of the house and jumped into Hood's Chevy Caprice. Hood pulled off, not knowing how close the streets were watching.

Detective Lawson sat at the end of the block in an unmarked Ford Taurus. When the detective working the case involving Blaze got the email regarding the connections Lawson linked together, he got a response. The information he received led him to this certain sector of Edgewood. As he sipped his hot coffee, he watched the house as Hood Ru and Tez-mo walked inside. He had nothing but time to figure out the connection they have to Simfany. He wasn't absolutely sure but he had a gut feeling that one of these Tree Top Piru members had something to do with Simfany being shot. The blue flag was the throw-off, and it would have probably continued a mystery but it happened twice at two shooting crime scenes. There had to be a connection. A thought arose as he sat in his Taurus. Lawson sat the coffee down in the divider and pulled out his cell phone to call his partner. Ramos answered after the first ring.

"Talk to me. What's up?"

"Question. What part of the county did Byrd set up shop in?" Lawson asked.

"Hold on, let me check the data base." Detective Lawson could hear Ramos type rapidly on the other end of the line.

"Here it is—Edgewood. It says he was connected to a person by the name of Hassan Jamir. He is a known drug dealer in Harford County. He goes by the alias of Hood Ru. But all that connects them is the county and that they were seen together on different occasions. Why? What are you up to?" Detective Ramos finally asked.

''Nothing, I'm at home. I was just reading this e-mail from the detectives out there. I can't seem to piece shit together with these bastards," Lawson lied.

"If you think of something, you call me. If you need me to look anything else up, I'll be at my desk until 2:00 pm." "I should be good. I was just wondering. Thank you though, partner," Lawson said jokingly.

"Yeah, whatever, smart ass." Ramos laughed then hung up. *Hassan Jamir.* As he looked out the window of his unmarked car, he wondered to himself which one of the members was Hassan Jamir. The nickname proved his suspicions. Byrd was connected to the gang in more ways than one. He just didn't know in what exact aspect it was.

Lawson sat up when the two men came out of the town house. "Where are we going so early?" he asked no one in particular. He put the Taurus in to *drive* and waited on the pair. The bubble Caprice pulled out; Lawson followed at a safe distance to maintain his cover.

***

Simfany rode through East Baltimore looking for any sight of Jimdog's maroon Crown Vic, with a pistol on her lap as she drove. She cruised through all the spots Byrd took her through, but still no sign of Jimdog or his maroon Vic. She had to revert to her only option left.

She picked up her cell phone out of the divider and placed a call.

"Yes, Simfany? What is the pleasure of hearing from you twice in one month? Is there a problem?" the groggy voice on the other end asked.

"Carlos, call Jimdog. Tell him I'm in the city and I'm trying to squash this shit. If he wants, I can come to him. This shit needs to stop."

"Not smart, Bonita, I can only hold the young man back so much. Please go back to your home. He won't bother you there. But if—" Simfany cut him off.

"You can't guarantee that, Carlos, because he already has come and made me uncomfortable. All I want to do is squash this beef. Call him, and then call me back. Please." She hung the phone up before Carlos had a chance to say anything further. She just hoped he made the call.

Subconsciously, Simfany rode through her old neighborhood, Edmonson and Carey. The scene was the same. Dope addicts, block boys, and prostitutes. Nothing ever changes about a city. It only gets worse. But she was glad she moved off Edmonson Avenue. The violence that occurred around the block would have been too much for Santana to avoid. She drove past Edmonson, awaiting a call from Carlos. She hadn't been in the city but twice since she was shot, and that was only to move her things and pick Santana up from Mitchell Courthouse. As she hit on Pennsylvania Avenue, she saw the blue light cameras at the end of every street corner. She remembered when the commissioner first put them in place. The violence only seemed to peak. It held its name well, Body More Murda Land. As she drove up Pennsylvania, her phone vibrated. Without taking her eyes off the road she felt around inside the divider with her right hand until she had her phone gripped in her hand.

"Yeah," she answered without looking her screen.

"Pretty lady, I'm 'bout to go to the Commons to take my mind off of shorty. Piru just called and said Hood and Stacks was on their way to come and pick me up. I just wanted to let you know," Santana explained.

"You said Hood and who?" she asked.

"The nigga Stacks I was telling you about the other night. The top, remember?" He talked over the music that was playing in the background. Simfany's heart pace quickened; the strange thing was she didn't know why. *What could the name mean that brought so much fear through her body.* She had no answers for herself.

"A'ight, you just make sure you be safe. You good though, right?" she asked.

"Yeah, all ten," Santana answered, understanding her concern. "Love you, Tana."

"Love you too, pretty lady." They ended the call, but her body was still trembling. The name meant nothing to her. She didn't know anyone by that here in Baltimore or in New York. That's what she couldn't understand. She remembered when Santana tried to explain the importance of the roles Stacks and Hood played, but still it meant nothing at the time. She didn't understand why her body was reacting this way now and not back then too. She was shaking too badly to drive. She pulled over near another car and double parked. Simfany had to get control of her nerves. It was a must; she knew, especially trying to see Jimdog. Her emotions had to be in check. She took a deep breath then exhaled. Simfany completed the pattern for about five minutes until she felt her nerves calm some. *What the fuck!* she thought. She took another deep breath and sighed. She looked out the window to her left and waited her turn to pull back into traffic.

As Simfany sat and waited for the light to change, her phone vibrated in the divider. She picked the phone up and answered it.

"Hello?"

"Jimdog said he'll meet you. I told him if you get hurt, he gets hurt—Please, mama, be safe," Carlos said flatly.

"I'm not the one you got to worry about, he is. My question to you is, if he gets hurt do I get hurt?" she asked as she pulled off as the light turned green. Carlos remained silent for a second too long before he answered.

"Listen, Simfany, I can't stop you or tell you what to do. But think about the consequences besides me. You're too beautiful to do time—"

She cut in; he was beating around the bush.

"Fuck the law, Carlos, do I have to hide from you again?"

"You never had to hide from me, mami, I take offense to that. I wanted to talk; nothing more, nothing less. The information was important to me. You know how I felt about Byrd." Carlos sighed. "But Jimdog don't have the same love. I put him on to keep him close to see what moves he make."

"Where does he want to meet me?"

"Monument and Port."

"I know where that it's at. Thank you, Carlos."

"Don't thank me, just go home. The same thoughts you feel about him, he may feel about you. I can send Jesus to you to make sure all goes well, your call."

"Nah, I'm good. All I 'm gone do is holla at the little boy. I'm okay, I promise," she replied as she gripped the gun that rested on her lap.

"He's riding with one of his friends today, so watch for him also. The last time I saw him he was in a white Altima. Again, be safe, Simfany," Carlos said. Simfany ended the call. Her adrenaline was rushing. After the night with the situation with Santana, she thought long and hard. She was tired of being the one looked for. It was life or death, and she refused to die or let her son die because of her. Meeting with Jimdog gave her motivation. He only had two options: leave them alone or die on the spot. Simfany sped to the freeway with murder on her mind. She hopped on I-95; Monument and Port was her next destination.

***

Detective Lawson followed the cherry red Caprice on to Hanson Road. The only two cars on the road were theirs. Lawson had no choice but to drive past them to elude suspicion. *It was okay,* he thought. The Caprice's left blinker came on, signaling the turn into a housing complex.

Lawson read the sign: *Windsor Valley Apartments.* He looked through his rear-view mirror as the car turned into the complex. Lawson looked up ahead for a place to turn around. A fire station was located on the far left side; he pulled into the turning lane in the middle of the road. He waited for the oncoming cars to pass. Lawson made the fire station's garage a means to make a U-turn. Lawson grew impatient as a new set of cars passed.

"Hurry the fuck up!" he yelled. He had a bad feeling that the Caprice would be gone by the time he got into the complex. When the last car passed, Lawson pulled on to Hanson Road. He made the right on to Meadowood Drive. He drove slowly up the short hill. The street sign read *Meadowood Court*. He looked at some of the parked cars along the block; there was no sign of the cherry red Caprice. So, Lawson continued down the road slowly at a moderate speed. He wasn't trying to bring attention to himself. Before he made it completely down the hill, he spotted the Caprice to his right. He slowed down to a crawl as he passed. He noticed the two men were still in the car. "They're waiting for somebody," he told himself. Just as soon as the words came out of his mouth the door to a town house opened. The person that ran out the house took Lawson for a loop. His theory had shattered right before his eyes. He put his foot on the gas to gain speed. Lawson made the next left and pulled into *Ironwood Court*. He had to digest it all; it was starting to get confusing. *What is Santana Vasquez doing with the people that might have shot his mother?* It would be a frequent question with no explanation. He sat in car and pulled out a cigarette. He had to calm his nerves.

The Caprice pulled out of the residential parking space and pulled onto the main road, leaving the complex. Lawson played the back and followed what he thought was a safe distance. What he was getting tired of was the cat and mouse game. Seeing his case go down ignited a fire deep inside his bones.

"Ock, is it me or is that Taurus following us? I been seeing that shit all morning," Hood, said looking through his rear-view mirror. Santana turned around in his seat. He recognized the face but couldn't place it. Hood drove down route 24 and hit Tremble Road, arriving in the Commons only a minute or so later. The Ford Taurus still in tow as they parked. The car slowed down a little but continued down the block. It was like he wanted them to know all eyes were on them. All three men exited the car and walked into the white town house that sat lonely at the corner. Piru and Tez-mo were arguing over the game as the niggas entered the room.

"Nigga, play defense. Stop letting the computer guard me, shorty!" Tez-mo complained.

"Blood, they're a part of my team and I got the joystick. I can use my niggas how I want!" Piru argued back. Santana laughed as the pair bickered back and forth. It brought back those old Hickey memories. He promised himself that he would write Drew. He sat down at the end of the table. Piru paused the game and looked at him.

"Damn, Ru, no love?" Piru asked Santana.

"My bad, my G, my shorty got my head fucked up. Plus, I saw you and Tez over there acting up," he said, getting out of his chair to peace both Tez-mo and Piru.

"I was about to say, blood, I got a Dutch and jar of that good-good for you on the table. Go ahead and twist two for the hood," Piru said as he turned back to the game. Santana went over to the table and grabbed two jars. He then walked to over where Hood sat and handed him the jars.

"Fuck you want me to do with this shit, ock?" Hood looked at Santana's stretched out hand.

"Nigga, roll it—Y'all niggas know I don't know how to roll," he said embarrassingly. Hood burst out laughing. Stacks just sat and observed Santana's demeanor.

"Give me, lor nigga." Hood grabbed for the weed. "Get the blunts too." Santana went and retrieved the box of *Dutch Masters.*

Stacks spoke. "So, what's poppin', shorty? You a'ight. Heard you had a lor issue the other night."

"Yeah, sort of. How you know about that?" Santana asked suspiciously.

"I run this city, my nigga. I know everything." Santana paid no attention to that big boy bullshit because he knew anybody could get smoked. Nobody was untouchable. His father was the perfect example.

"Anyway, a nigga I had beef within the city came down and rained shots. But of course, with no success. I'm good, though."

"That's what's good. Hold it down then. The issue not dead then I assume. And if not, what can I do to help?" Stacks asked sincerely.

"Nothing, I'm good. That beef will never be over until one of us dead. The nigga laid hands on my lady. It's on sight with me."

Stacks gave Santana a disapproving look. "All this over a broad, lor yo? It's too many lor breezy's out there to die over."

Santana laughed. "Nah, I'm not beefing over no pussy, my G. I'm beefing over the fact shorty put his hands on my mother. So, you already know what it is with me." Stacks nodded, letting him know he understood. Hood looked over at Stacks; they knew what the other was thinking.

Stacks tried reassuring Santana. "Whatever the situation, you need us, we're there. And don't be afraid to ask, shorty. We a family, we got you."

"Good looking, *five*, the love the same on this end."

Hood lit the blunt in his mouth. The room grew an awkward silence. Stacks sat back and thought. Hood lit the second blunt. Piru and Tez-mo continued to argue over who was better at the game. Santana just sat there and blew his mind out. Santana broke the silence.

"Hood, remember when I called you the other night to ask where you was?"

"Yeah, I think you talking 'bout the night we was at the Docks."

"I just remembered the nigga that dumped on me tried to use your name to get me to come to him. I'm not sure but the nigga called me ock and everything."

"What's the nigga name?" Hood looked at Santana with confusion written all over his face.

"The nigga's name is Jimdog. He from over east," Santana explained. He looked at Hood to see if the name brought any sign of recognition. None. Santana looked around the room; nobody else seemed to be paying attention. He left Byrd's name out of it because he knew they knew him; he wasn't trying to connect the dots for them. He just wanted to see what their facial expressions would be like.

"Never heard of the young bull. He must know somebody from out here if he know, how I talk. Or he might just know some other Philly niggas." Hood began putting two and two together. "Hold up, you thought it was me that was dumping at you?"

"Nah, I knew it wasn't you. The accent was different. But I called to make sure. I would be dumb not to. I was really calling you to tell you that son was using your name. But on blood I never once thought it was you that banged on me." Santana lied. He didn't know if they had the same connection with Jimdog as they had with Byrd. He couldn't leave no stone unturned. Especially not when it came to life and death.

"That's crazy though, this nigga drawn for real," Hood said, talking to no one in particular. Santana sat and looked Hood over. He wanted answers about the Harford Square situation.

"Yo, Ru, whatever happened to the nigga in the square that night?" Santana asked.

"Aw, you speaking on the boy Nelo." Hood laughed, knowing this conversation would eventually take place. It only confirmed his suspicions that Santana was a killer. Wanting to know about confirmed kills just shows a different kind of level of shooting guns. Hood continued. "The bullets you fired were blanks, ock," Hood explained. The look on Santana's face told it all; he was disappointed.

"So, I didn't body that nigga?" Hood shook his head.

"My nigga, I seen the blood gush from his face though. That pussy should be dead!" Santana grabbed everybody in the room's attention. Piru looked at him with a knowing glance. He was proud of him; that he knew for sure. Piru and Tez-mo turned back around to play the game, but Stacks on the other hand looked on without speaking a word.

"Listen, ock, the nigga Nelo alive and well. Shook up. but alive. I'm guessing the bark from the first shot caused the window to shatter, cutting the lame nigga's face. That doesn't matter though. What matters is you proved your loyalty. I now understand without hesitation where your loyalty lies. But believe this, there won't be no more blanks in your gun. You got a lot of heart to be as young as you are. Piru speak highly you, but not all the time does that heart pan out. Meaning you might be a fighter but won't bust a nigga's head. From *my* understanding you will do both. Take this as a lesson, ock, test niggas before you give them your loyalty. Even me, the odds stay stacked against us, lor bro, so never and I mean *never* get complacent and always hold it down." Hood exclaimed and threw up his set. Santana sat and listened, taking every word to heart and storing it in his memory bank. He realized that they had love for him, and he also had love for them. But what he wouldn't confuse that love with was the love he has for his one and only, Simfany, his mother. Every day that Santana woke up he reminded himself no matter how much love he claims he had for the five, it couldn't and wouldn't add up to the love he held for his mother. It was truly hard not to get caught up with them niggas, but what pushed him forward was the knowledge that one of them shot Simfany. He tried hard not to lose focus. He was patient. Only time would tell who the shooter was, he hoped at least. He re-lit the blunt and smoked to the possibility of revenge. He laid back and smiled, thinking about the day the person that shot his mother drew his last breath.

***

Simfany turned onto Monument and Port in search of a white Altima. She brought the Durango to a creep as she spotted the Altima. She looked around for a spot to park and pulled over. The car looked empty. She might have been paranoid, but the car was parked in her direction. She had to look around at the other cars to make sure she wasn't the one parked the wrong way. She wasn't the Altima was. Simfany looked over the row of homes that rested on the block. She was mainly concentrated on the row of homes that the Altima was sitting in front of. She sat and stood for somebody to come out and get her. Each second that passed by, she became more and more anxious. Still, nobody showed up. She thought about calling Carlos again but she didn't want that to become a habit, so she just chilled and waited. Simfany reached into her lap and put the gun she had rested there under her seat for easy access if needed. As she came back up from under the seat, a gun was trained on her head outside of her window. Simfany refused to look over.

"Open up ya window shorty!" the boy shouted over the window. Simfany pushed the electric button on the panel to roll the window down. The cold breeze made her shiver. She was scared, but she refused to show it. When she looked out the window and past the gun, all she saw was a child, a child not much younger than Santana covered in tattoos in all visible paces. The ones that caught her attention most were the two tear drops he had under his right eye. In the life they lived, it meant murder. It was a message to the streets of the bodies he caught. The youngin spoke again.

"You the breezy that's supposed to be here for Jimdog?"

"Yes. But I don't know where to look, I—" she was cut off.

"Hold on. I'm gone call him outside." The boy pulled out his phone and dialed the number, but still had his gun drawn.

"Yeah, dog. Shorty out here—Nah, she in a black Durango. Yeah, that's her." He stopped talking and looked into the window, observing the interior of the car. The boy didn't put much effort into looking in the Durango.

"Nah, yo, she don't look strapped—A'ight. I'm out here." He ended the call and tucked his gun into his waist band at the same time. She sighed; the initial threat was over. No words were further exchanged between the two.

Simfany watched as a figure walked out of the town house she was just studying moments before. She smiled at herself for guessing the right house. As the figure approached, she thought she was looking at a ghost. It was Byrd. Or she thought it was anyway. As the man got closer, more and more of Byrd faded away. It was Jimdog. His whole appearance was different, he looked like money, she had to admit, plus the boy was sexy.

Jimdog walked over to the passenger side door and waited to hear the locks click. Simfany hit the automatic locks so Jimdog could get in the car. Before he entered, he looked over the hood and she heard him say:

"I'm good, shorty, go start the whip. After this we gone slide back to your spot." The kid walked off and jumped into the driver side of the white Altima, bringing it to life.

Jimdog sat down and closed the door.

"So, what's up, Simfany?" Jimdog smiled, showing his white gold fronts. *The little nigga came up, I see.*

"Please don't play games with me, Jimdog. If you got a problem with me let's leave it between us. Leave my son out of this."

"You know what's funny is, I don't have a problem with you shorty. But ya son, ya lor nigga tried to end me. So, let's not play stupid about what it is." Jimdog pulled his gun off his waist, sitting it on his lap. Simfany's heart jumped and sped a million miles per hour. She was scared to death. She now regretted the decision to come down and talk to Jimdog.

"That's unnecessary," she said, nodding at the gun.

"I'm not going to hurt you. Carlos made that clear, but shorty, I gotta make sure I'm good too." He checked around the car for a gun. He checked everywhere, leaving no spot unchecked, except one, under the driver side seat. He never once attempted to lean over and check.

"What are you doing?"

"Checking to make sure you don't have any weapons preferably that Glock you always carry."

"Why would you check the divider though, the gun would hang out, don't you think?" Jimdog shrugged. She felt like it was more to it than that. It was like he was warned to check that spot. She spoke her mind. "Nah, Jimdog. You knew where I kept my gun. But who told you?"

"I got my ways, Simfany. But that's not important. Why do you want to talk to me besides about lor yo?"

"I swear it's over with, Jimdog. Please just leave my son alone. I'll pay you if need be. It don't matter what you want. I can give it to you. My son shot you because he was trying to protect me. He has no problems with you personally. The only beef is coming from your side of the tracks."

"I couldn't tell. I gotta admit ya lor shorty grown up into a lor monster. Most niggas run for their life when they get dumped on. Not this lor nigga, he started to bust back. I respect his G. You gotta understand, Simfany, that beef will never be over. Santana almost killed me, so it's time to return the favor. No matter where I see the

150

lor nigga he gone hold what I got in my clip." He was talking reckless, thinking there really weren't any consequences. Simfany
stared at Jimdog angrily. Hearing him talk about killing Santana
made her feel some type of way. She had no choice but to keep her
comments to herself, after all he was the one with the advantage.

"Then it's nothing more I can say, but you try to kill him, you
might as well kill me," she replied.

"I'd hate to do that. You're too beautiful to play with fire like
that. And to be honest the only reason you're not laid in a morgue
is because of Carlos. But again, we'll meet soon. I hope."

Jimdog smiled. He opened the door and got out. The white Altima spun around, going the right way. The car waited in the middle
of the street for Jimdog to hop into the passenger seat.

Simfany nervously reached under her seat and grabbed her gun.
She sat it back on her lap. It bothered her that he knew about where
she kept her gun when she was in her car. Only a few people had
been in her car. Byrd was one of those people. She couldn't see him
going out his way to tell Jimdog that. Not only did he know where
she kept her shit, he knew what kind of gun she had. She watched
Jimdog walk across the street and hop into the waiting car. The car
just sat there. Jimdog put his arm out the window, signaling for her
to pass.

Simfany put the Durango into drive and slowly crept up the
block. She pulled up the passenger side window, she rolled down
her window in one final attempt to talk to Jimdog and squash whatever beef he had. Jimdog rolled his window down.

"Jimdog, please!"

"Simfany, begging doesn't fit you." He smiled up at her. He
saw the fire grow behind her eyes, but he could care less. Simfany
tried to calm herself down. She gripped the handle of her Glock
tightly.

"I'm not asking for me or Santana no more. I'm asking for the
sake of both you and me."

"Then if that's the case, I'm good because I'm gone hunt ya lor
man until my body cold." The look he now saw in her eyes he knew
all too well, not because of himself but because of the niggas he was

associated with. He made a mental note to watch Simfany closely. She laughed.

She started to put the pieces together as she sat there and listened to Jimdog's bullshit ass spill.

"Be careful what you ask for, baby boy. Remember your brother taught me a lot. That's why I will always love him. As a matter of fact, tell him I send my love. Oh, and tell that bitch Paris she dead too."

"What you mean she dead too?" Jimdog asked, phone in hand, smiling, showing off his white gold teeth. Simfany raised the Glock out the window; the look on his face was that of shock before he tried to dive for cover. She pulled the trigger—*Boc—Boc—Boc— Boc*—shooting into the passenger side window. There was no way for him to escape. Each bullet that pierced his body sent him closer and closer to hell. Simfany aimed higher in hopes of killing the kid that was riding with him. Boc—Boc—Boc—the bullet holes made metal imprints as the bullets entered the car. Simfany emptied the rest of the clip into the Altima within seconds and sped off, leaving Jimdog and his little man in the hands of the grim reaper.

Chapter Fifteen

Simfany pulled into her residential parking spot. Any evidence that could link her to *Enterprise*, she got rid of. She cleaned her Tahoe, making sure nothing was suspicious or out of place. Killing Jimdog took a major burden off both her and Santana's shoulder. The young kid Jimdog was with is what hurt her. She didn't know if she killed him too; the sad part is she hoped so. He was the only one that could place her there besides Carlos. And she knew Carlos wouldn't even mention he had knowledge of the meeting. So, at the moment she was safe, she hoped. Regardless of the fact she felt she may have got away with murder again, something was still bothering her. She couldn't put her finger on it, but she knew it was something. *Fuck it,* she thought. One person she wanted to see was the little bitch, Paris. Tijuana had hit the bull on the head when she said Paris was probably on some grimy shit. Being a female, she gave the little bitch the benefit of a doubt.

Simfany walked into the house and dropped Santana's sneakers at the base of the steps. Her business wasn't over just yet. Paris was now an important piece to the puzzle. She wanted the dots connected a little more before she could move on. Simfany searched her contact list for Paris's number, but she realized she never cared to save the girl's number. Simfany strolled down to Santana's number and pressed the send button to place the call.

"What's up?" he answered after a couple rings.

"What's Paris's number?" Simfany asked. Santana spit the number off the *top* of his head.

"Good looking, Tana, and tell Piru I'm gone whoop his ass if he gives you any more weed!" Simfany laughed but was dead serious. She could hear in her son's speech he was high.

"I love you, pretty lady," he replied.

"Love you too, boy, I'm serious. You can't stay on point if you high all the time. Don't start to get comfortable, little nigga." Santana said nothing because he knew what she said was true. The silence was enough to signal the end of the conversation. Simfany didn't want to hear any lies or excuses, so she hung up, giving Santana something to think about. She hurried and placed her call to Paris. The phone call was brief. Simfany asked Paris to come over to talk about Santana. At first it sounded as if Paris was reluctant to come but agreed none the less. Ten minutes later Simfany heard a knock at the door while she sat in the kitchen waiting for Paris.

"Come in," she called from the kitchen. From where Simfany sat she could see the whole view of the door. Simfany stood as the door opened, Glock behind her back as she approached the opening door. Paris came in, but not alone. She held the hand of a bundled up little girl. Simfany tucked the gun in the small of her back. She was taken by surprise with this one, she had to admit. After Paris unbuttoned the baby's coat, Paris sat the child in front of the television and turned to the Cartoon Network. It would hold the child's attention for a while. Simfany nodded to the kitchen. Paris followed. Neither woman took a seat. It was hostility all in the air. Simfany sensed the tension.

"Paris, who is that little girl?" she asked curiously.

"That's my daughter." That took Simfany a minute to digest.

"Your daughter? I never knew you had a child. Does Santana know?"

"No, but of course it's no secret. You called me over here to talk about something, and I know it's not about Santana. So, speak what's on ya mind, Ms. Vasquez." Her cool attitude told Simfany that in fact she really knew why she was over there.

"I thought you had love for us, ma, what made you want to kill us? And please don't lie. I know and you know I do. But when did you know I figured it out?" Simfany asked Paris.

"I do love your son—"

"Bitch! Stop playing with me. Now tell me why the fuck you want me and my son dead!" she yelled at Paris. Paris looked into the living room at her daughter; she was engrossed in Sponge Bob Square Pants.

"Hello! Do you fucking hear me, Paris?"

Paris replied coolly: "Simfany, you don't have to yell at me. I know exactly what you want to hear. How about this? I can call the police and tell them you may have just killed Jimdog and his friend, or you can lower your voice and hear me out. You choose." Simfany took the gun from the small of her back and pointed the barrel at Paris's head.

"How about I just push ya dreads back, you little bitch! And for the record I didn't kill anybody. But what you will do is tell me how you know that bitch ass nigga Jimdog and why the fuck you tried to set us up!" Simfany's emotions started to get the best of her. Paris's whole demeanor changed when she saw Simfany wasn't about to fold to her threat.

"Simfany, I don't want to die, please put the gun away. My lor girl keeps looking over here. Please, Simfany, put the gun away." Paris finally understood the danger she was placed in. Paris cried; bringing her daughter with her proved also to be a mistake. But Paris knew if she came alone, she would probably be dead by now. *Fuck, she cursed herself for even coming at all.* Simfany looked at Paris then looked into the living room at the precious little girl staring innocently back at her. Simfany lowered her gun.

"Paris, begin. Start from the beginning."

"Okay. Remember when you lived in Havre De Grace. Well so did I. Me and my momma lived only a couple houses down from your friend Carol. I was too young for you to remember and I didn't have dreads then. I remember you, you know why, because I always envied your beauty, especially at your age. No disrespect." Simfany stared at Paris, amazed. *How could death be so close and I didn't know it?* Simfany thought. Paris continued. "Hill Top is where I met Jimmy. Jimdog, as you and Santana call him. The boy was sexy, I fell in love with him. Only a couple months later I found out I was pregnant with Shakira. Jimmy took care of me the whole pregnancy.

Eventually you moved, but still I knew nothing of your connection to my baby's father. Jimmy asked me to move out here to Edgewood, and of course I did. But it was like once I got out here, his true colors came to light. Still, I rocked with the nigga hard. He put me out here to give him a place to stay at when he came in from the city. I couldn't complain. He put food in my mouth, paid the bills, and when he did stay over, he made me feel loved. But as the time passed, he barely came around. Even when I had Shakira his presence was slim. So, I moved my mother out here with me to help care for my daughter. A lot of people assume Shakira is my mother's baby. I let people think what they want. It keeps me out the rumor mill."

"But where did we cut into your world and where did the hate come from?" Simfany asked.

"Please let me finish. You asked from the beginning. You'll understand better at the end." Simfany sat down and looked at Paris. She nodded, giving Paris the go-ahead to spill away.

"Anyway, the only connection I had to Jimmy in the last year was the money he sent for Shakira, and he sent that in way of *Western Union*. But then all of a sudden, he started to pop back up on an everyday basis. That was around the time Santana had got out. I never put two and two together until the night Santana came home and said what kind of car shot at him. I was scared that not only would y'all hate me because that was my daughter's father, but I was scared that I would die. After that night I made Jimmy tell me about the beef between him and Santana.

At first, I thought it was because of me of course, but deep down I knew better. It was deeper than me. That's when I realized that me and my daughter were just pawns on Jimmy's chess board. We meant nothing to that nigga. I was gone tell Santana everything I knew, but then he started accusing me of setting him up. I got scared to say anything. I just fell in love with the wrong set of niggas." Paris looked over at Simfany with tears streaking down her face. What she said was sincere; she just hoped Simfany didn't think she was lying.

Simfany had a lot of questions, and she wanted all them answered. The tears running down Paris face meant nothing to her.

"So how did the nigga know about my guns and where I put them? Only you can tell that. So why did you?" Simfany asked.

"I did tell him that, but I only asked why you always carried the gun everywhere you went. Jimmy acted like he knew you from Havre De Grace so I asked him why. That was before I knew what was really going on though." Paris explained.

"Did he ever ask about Santana?"

"No, that's how he kept me out the loop. He never showed any interest in him. He seemed to hold some level of respect for you, Simfany. He told me about you and his older brother."

"Okay, well, then remember that night we went out, he was behind us, right? Why didn't you tell me who it was then?"

"I didn't know he bought that car until days later. I only knew because he came to my house that same week. I never paid attention to the kind of car he drove until the shit was too deep to get out of. I told you I put everything together the night Santana was shot at.''

"Why did you call Santana at the time Jimdog was looking for him?"

"I was calling to tell him to pick up some extra chicken for me, but I was really gone take it home to Shakira. Plus, a bitch was hungry after I burnt that steak. Simfany, I understand that a lot of this shit doesn't add up to the right picture, but I swear woman to woman, I love you and your son with all my heart. I was put in the middle of a war I didn't even have knowledge of. Everything I said this morning I meant. I can't be around here if y'all think I'm the enemy. I won't feel safe if there's no trust. How you and Santana carry them guns around, you would think we lived in Pakistan. Man, I don't know, just ask yourself if you was put in my position what would you do?" Paris asked.

The question hung in the air. If Dracula had put her through that, she didn't know what she would have done. One thing she knew for sure, she would have his back. Even if she was at odds with the nigga, she would at least hold his secrets. So, half of her didn't blame Paris, but another half was mad because they weren't warned.

"Simfany, you gone say anything?" Paris asked nervously.

"What can I say? If what you're saying is true, he used you and your family to get to me and mine. It was just by chance that Santana happened to fall in love with *you*. I done seen weird shit, but this takes the cake. Fate is a muthafucka. Paris, due to the fact that your baby daddy can no longer harm me or my son, I will give you the benefit of a doubt that you got caught up in a fucked-up ordeal. But

I swear on my life—I find out you lied to me, I'm gone come and see you. But you a'ight with me, I guess. Me being a woman that was in love with a real nigga, I can understand some of where you got caught up in the bullshit. But Santana has to form his own opinion of the situation." The look of fear appeared on Paris's face again. She didn't want to have this conversation with Santana.

"Calm down. If you want to be with him, you will have to explain. If you're going to move on, the situation stays with me. Those are your only two options."

"I understand. What about Jimmy? They will come to you first because of your past troubles."

"I still don't know what you're talking about, Paris. I have no knowledge of them boys being killed. I was at home." "I know you were with me all morning." Paris gazed into the living room at Shakira dancing to a song that played on TV. She smiled at her daughter's innocence. *Another child growing up without a father,* she thought. Paris had to remind herself often that Jimdog wasn't ever around anyway. The money was okay but being around was what Shakira needed. The love she once held for Jimdog turned into anger and hatred over the years. It was sad he was gunned down, but she wouldn't miss him.

"Paris, you don't have drag yourself into this, I'm okay," Simfany reassured her.

"Nah, I feel like this the only way I can make up for the bullshit that went on. I want you to trust me again. I got a lot of love and respect for you. I envy the love you and Santana have for each other. My mother is totally different from you. I was always taught to protect the people you love. So, like I said, I was with you all day, me and Shakira. I got you if you need me. I swear."

"Why you think I killed them, Paris?" Simfany had to ask.

"I know for a fact you did, Simfany. I even heard every last word you said before you pulled the trigger."

"And how do you figure that? And if so tell me what I said." Simfany didn't believe her.

"Hear it for yourself." Paris pulled out her cell phone and placed it on speaker. She called her voicemail. The automated voice messaging system came up. Within seconds Simfany could hear Jimdog's voice leaving a message for Paris to call him about Shakira, but the call obviously was over. All she heard was shuffling at first, only seconds later Simfany recognized her own voice pleading with Jimdog for him to leave her and Santana alone. It even had the part clear as day to tell Paris she would be dead next and then multiple shots could be heard through the receiver. The panic in the car was also heard, the message cut off. Before Simfany could speak, Paris pressed *four* deleting the message forever.

"Why you do that?" Simfany asked, dumbfounded over her luck. If the DA got a hold of that message, she would never see the light of day again. The message was crucial; it was a way for Simfany to play fair. Still, Paris deleted the message without a second thought. Simfany was stuck; she didn't know how to feel for real.

"I didn't love him no more, Simfany. He never loved me. But to be honest that was never my issue, I could care less if he loved me, and all I wanted was for him to love his daughter. But it was too hard for him. He loved nobody but his brother and himself." Paris dropped her head. She lifted her head, eyes wet from her thoughts. She continued. "He never loved either one of *us*. Like I said before, I was only a pawn. Karma is a muthafucka, you know. I want you to trust me again. I meant no harm, and I'm sorry for not keeping it real from the beginning. Fear makes people do things you wouldn't normally do. Please forgive me." Paris begged using the puppy dog eyes. Simfany busted out laughing. Paris turned beet red.

"Ma, who taught you that face? I bet it's Santana. He could con anybody with that face back in the day. Unfortunately, those puppy eyes no longer work against me. I forgive you, but my statement still stands. As long as you didn't lie, we are cool. Now Santana— that's another story. I won't get involved, but you will have to tell him, or I will. Come here." Simfany opened up her arms and Paris came into her embrace. Paris lost herself and started crying. She was crying for herself, for Jimdog, for betraying Simfany and Santana's trust. She just cried for all that happened in the last couple months of her life. All Simfany could do was offer her shoulder for Paris to cry on.

Both women were so caught up in the moment they didn't hear Santana come through the door. Santana walked through the door; he saw his mother hugging a crying Paris. He was still high from the weed he blew earlier. He wasn't in the mood for family reunions, especially not now. Truth be told, he was happy to see Paris, but what could he say to her now, he wondered. He already said what he felt was needed to be said. Words couldn't explain how sorry he was. But he wouldn't keep dwelling on the situation. He slammed the door and kicked off his shoes. He grabbed the bag at the foot of the steps and went into the living room. He stopped short when he saw the little girl sitting in front of the television watching cartoons. *Who the fuck is that?* he asked himself. It was as if the child felt his presence and looked up.

"Tana," she called out. He laughed. It sounded like she was saying *Santa*. She lifted her arms for him to pick her up.

"My pleasure, baby girl," he said as he bent down and lifted Shakira into his arms. Santana walked into the kitchen with Shakira in his arms. He waited for the emotional ordeal to end, or tried to, at least.

"Mommy," Shakira said in a sing-song kind of voice. Simfany opened her eyes. *Oh shit,* Simfany thought to herself. Before Simfany could give warning, Paris answered:

"Yes, baby." Paris turned around not to two eyes staring back at her; it was four. Paris felt as if her heart was going to stop when she saw Santana holding Shakira. Simfany looked at Paris, Paris looked at Santana. The tension built, but still no one said anything.

Simfany got up and reached for Shakira. The pair left, leaving Santana and Paris alone in the kitchen. Santana sat down.

"So, what's up? That's your daughter?" Paris nodded. She couldn't even look him in his eyes. She didn't know how to tell him everything. He was a man; he would show no sympathy that she knew, but she had to tell him. Paris took a seat also across from him.

"So, what do you wanna hear first? The good news or the bad news?"

"What you mean, my nigga?"

"I don't want to argue, Santana, at all, okay. But good or bad first?"

"Good," he finally answered.

"Jimdog was killed this morning in the city." The smile that rose on his face told a story of its own. A calm look came over him.

"So, what's the bad news?" he asked curiously. Paris took a second to choose her words wisely. There was really no good way to put it.

"Jimdog was my daughter's father. But—" she tried to explain.

"Fuck you mean, Paris? You been fucking this nigga and pillow-talking about my casket!"

He was vexed. "What the fuck type shit you on, my nigga! You know what, shorty, get the fuck out of my house." He stood.

"Santana, please let me explain. I swear it wasn't—"

"Get the fuck out of my house!" Paris's eyes watered.

"Please, baby, I'm not against you. Let me explain. God damn it!" Paris yelled back. The shouting made Shakira begin to cry in the other room. Simfany walked into the kitchen and glared at Santana.

"Let her talk, then you judge her. But first hear her out and please keep it down. You're scaring the baby." Simfany walked into the kitchen with Shakira in tow. Paris looked down at her daughter.

"I'm okay, beautiful, me and Tana just playing a game," Paris told her daughter softly. She wiped her eyes and kissed Shakira on her head. When Simfany was about leaving the kitchen, Shakira whined and threw her arms out to Santana. She wanted him. He got up and took her into his arms. He sat back down in his seat. Shakira tugged on his hair as he held on to her. When she finally got the hair she wanted, she laid her head on his chest, put her two fingers in her mouth and played with his hair with her other hand. Simfany gave both of them the look to be civil while Shakira was present. She left the kitchen and went upstairs. Santana glared at Paris. He was mad and he didn't even know the half. The name alone made him furious. He wanted to know why she did him like that.

"Why, Paris? Why would you do this to somebody that loves you?" he finally spoke.

"Please let me explain and hopefully you will understand. Your mother did, hopefully you will also." Santana said nothing. He looked down at the precious little girl rested on his chest. She was falling asleep; he rocked back and forth. Shakira closed her eyes. She let go of his hair and curled up to her comfort.

"Please explain, ma," Santana simply stated. Paris explained the same exact story except the part about Simfany being the shooter. The look that he displayed shot daggers through her soul. She knew he wouldn't understand; that was written all over her face. He just watched Shakira's chest rise and fall as she slept.

"Please say something, Santana, the silence is killing me." Paris looked at him.

"What made you tell me? My mother put it together, didn't she?" he asked already knowing the answer to his own question.

"Yeah, she called me over to talk about it, but I knew before I stepped foot in this house, I was gone tell all. I played no part in his fucking game, Santana. I myself put two and two together."

"So, if my mother didn't call you, you probably wouldn't be here?"

"Ask your mother about the message that was left on my voicemail this morning. I had no choice but to confront my demons. Your mother almost killed me in front of my daughter this morning. Still, I told her everything I knew. I can't see myself without you. As you can see, my baby girl loves you. She knows all about you. She thinks you're her father." Santana gave her a look.

"I never told her that. I just always tell her I love you and that your name is Santana. Every time she sees your picture, she says she loves you too. I would never put my child in harm's way. I love her more than I love you and myself, or anybody on the face of this earth for that matter. Just let me know how you feel. Please." Paris wiped her eyes. Once again, her eyes betrayed her. She couldn't stop the tears from coming. Santana looked down at Shakira and answered.

"I'm not mad at you, ma. If you didn't play a position in his game, I have no issues with you. But, just to be honest, trusting you will take some time. Regardless, though, I love you, ma. If it's meant to be, we will get through this. When he finished what he said, he didn't know if he forgave her because of what she told him or if it was because of the precious little angel sound asleep on his chest. No matter the reason, he was willing to forgive, but by no means would he ever forget.

Chapter Sixteen

Lawson pulled over on the shoulder of Route 24 to evaluate what he had just witnessed. Santana Vasquez, Hassan Jamir, Simfany Vasquez and Brian Parks had all been connected, but in this way. Shit was getting real. To solve his case was so demanding that he missed the most important facts. They stood in his face for so long. Yet, he believed one thing or another, causing him to make up his own facts. He adopted a false mental hope, just to have something to hold on to. He cursed himself. No matter how it looked, he knew he was on a right road at least. Lawson just didn't understand where he went astray. He hated to admit it, but he thought Ramos might have been right. *Nah, fuck that,* he thought.

"I know these bastards are connected. They won't cause mayhem and continue to get away with this shit." He said those words to nobody in particular. He lifted his head and pulled back onto Route 24, looking for new answers to his old questions.

Lawson drove and let his mind shift through why Santana would be with Hassan Jamir. Lawson was so lost in his thoughts; his phone rang and went unanswered. The call that went unanswered would change Santana's life forever.

***

Santana sat and thought about what he should do regarding Paris and Shakira. If he really believed her, he understood that she may have been caught up in some bullshit. He was fighting within himself whether or not would he be able to move on with her. Shakira still laid sound asleep on his chest. One thing he knew for sure, he would do his best to be there for Shakira even if he and Paris were no longer cool. What Santana didn't know was, Simfany was responsible for Jimdog being toe tagged. He had enough on his mind to keep him busy. His phone rang. He looked at it but thought against answering it. So, he didn't. He wasn't in the mood to talk to no one. He was stuck in between surviving and being in love. He weighed the pros and cons regarding the two. He shook that thought out of his head. He couldn't fall blind to the fact that she knew and he wasn't told. He genuinely forgave Paris, but he refused to be caught slipping again. Santana's phone rang again.

"You gone answer your phone, Santana?" Paris asked. He was so lost in thought he heard neither Paris nor his phone. "Santana!" Paris called. She woke up Shakira and got his attention.

"What's up, ma?"

"Ya phone is going crazy over there," Paris explained.

"Answer it then, I got little momma right now. Plus, you got a nigga's mind fucked up right now." Paris said nothing. There was nothing she really could say. Paris walked over and grabbed his phone. The phone stopped ringing as soon as she approached the counter.

"If it's important they'll call back," Santana replied.

"What's on ya mind? Talk to me. If we going to continue to be together, we must get back to what we used to be. I didn't betray you, Santana. After I found out about the beef between you and my baby daddy, I was scared to lose you—not him. So, I kept it to myself. Please don't hate me for that. I meant no harm. I love you, Santana. Shakira loves you. Before you begin to act like you love me but despise me, let me go. I want you. I want your heart to be pure. I—" Paris was cut off by the ringing of her own phone. Santana looked at Paris. Paris reached into her pocket and grabbed her phone.

"Hello—calm down—Piru, calm down. He's right here." Paris passed Santana the phone urgently. Santana's eyes asked the questions his mouth couldn't. Paris shrugged.

"Hello, who this?" Santana asked.

"Fuck all that, blood, get the fuck out that house. The police are squadding up to come get you!"

"Piru, what the fuck you talking about?"

"The gang unit on their way for a homicide. They already on Hanson, shorty, hurry up. I'll be in the square waiting on you."

"My nigga, calm down, you got to explain."

"Nigga, I don't have time. Get the fuck out that house now, lor nigga, and meet me in the square. Ru, leave now, shorty. The scanner going crazy. Nigga, leave the—" Santana could hear Piru get frustrated.

"Listen, ock, this Hood. The police trying book you for a body. They probably trying to surround ya spot right now. They say you bodied a nigga or some shit. You're their prime suspect. Get to the square, my nigga. We'll wrap about it then." Santana could hear the sirens in the distance. That told him he still had a chance to get away. He thought about it for a second. *But I didn't do anything,* he told himself. Santana looked up at a frightful Paris and Simfany. He woke up Shakira and handed her over to Paris.

"What are they talking about, Santana?" Simfany asked. He heard the sirens getting closer.

"Ma, I gotta rock. I'll try to explain later if I can. I love all three of y'all." He ran to his mother and kissed her. He kissed Shakira, and then hugged Paris.

"We love you, Tana," Paris whispered into his ear.

"I love you too, ma," he replied. He opened the screen door and looked back. All he could do was nod before he took off. He took off in hopes of making it to Harford Square.

Fuck did I do now? They said the nigga Nelo didn't die. He cursed himself as he sprinted through the complex to the wooded area that separated Meadowood from Harford Square.

***

Lawson sat in his Taurus waiting on the gas pump valve to click, indicating he had a full tank. As he waited, the police scanner came to life. They had a person of interest in a murder investigation. He listened intently. The officers were warned to proceed with caution. In laymen's terms that meant shoot to kill if need be because the suspect was armed and perceived to be dangerous. It was interesting to listen to; it made Lawson's adrenaline rush. He loved the action he got from being a cop. What he heard next caught his attention, the description of the suspect. He almost spilled his coffee, rummaging through his accumulated paperwork regarding the Vasquez and Parks family. He looked in his folder to make sure he wasn't tripping. He was just at 542 Meadowood Drive. That was the address he followed Hassan Jamir to. It was Santana's residence. Santana was wanted for a murder that happened at the same time he was following behind them. *That's luck for you,* he thought to himself. Lawson knew Santana couldn't have committed that crime. He picked his phone up to place a call to clear Santana's name. As he held Santana's fate in his hand, he looked at his phone. He saw that he had three missed calls. He put off the call to the station and called his voicemail. It was his partner, Detective Ramos.

"Lawson, I just called you at home, you little sneaky son of a bitch. Where are you? You need to answer your damn phone. I think you would like to know that Jimmy "Jimdog" Parks and Joseph Wells were gunned down today in Baltimore City on Monument and Port. If you get the chance call me back ASAP!" Lawson hung the phone up and hopped in his car. He wanted to be there when they arrested Santana. He couldn't let that child go down for something he didn't do. He was a true cop at heart, aside from the rush of danger. He sped off in hopes of getting to the scene on time.

Lawson got lost going up Hanson Road. He remembered the fire station that sat on the right of the road. What he couldn't remember was what turns he made, so he slowed and looked around. He could hear the sirens blaring, but he didn't see any cars. The cherry red Caprice that passed him caught his attention. It was the same car he followed earlier that day which Hassan Jamir drove. He began to follow the car again. He was hoping that Santana was in the car instead of at his home. He followed at a safe distance. The Caprice took a left turning into another complex he didn't remember going in earlier. On the left was a wooded area that separated the two complexes. The Caprice made the first right into a housing court. Lawson continued down the small hill. He stopped as he saw a figure running through the woods. The person looked frantic. Lawson parked his car on the road. He had to see what was going on with the Jamir kid.

Santana had to sit on the back burner for a second, he decided. He had a feeling that the revelation he was about to find cut was more important. But as the figure came fully out of the woods, he realized what was going on. Santana was running from the law. *Damn, this kid is stupid. Why would he run? He knows he didn't kill anybody. Man, fuck!* Without thinking, Lawson opened the door and got out of his car. He wanted to help the young man.

"Santana Vasquez!" Detective Lawson called out. Santana looked up and stopped his stride.

"Santana, you'll be okay, just come with me." Santana just stood and watched Lawson come closer.

"Come on, Santana, you'll be okay. I know you didn't kill any-body. Come on." Lawson tried to get Santana to come to him. *Don't be difficult, damn it,* he thought to himself as he inched closer to Santana.

Santana watched as the mysterious white man made his way towards him. *Who the fuck is this nigga, man?* He cursed himself. He looked past the man and looked at the car that was directly be-hind him. It was the same car that had followed him, Stacks and Hood Ru earlier that morning. He got nervous every step the white man took.

"Stop coming near me. My nigga, I don't know you. Stay away from me." Santana watched as Piru and Hood drove by. The look on Piru's face was menacing. The man was so engulfed in Santana he didn't see the Caprice make a U-turn. Santana touched his hip. His Glock was in place. If his thought was right, he knew what was most likely about to take place. The Caprice pulled up in front of the wooded area right in front of Santana.

"Hop in, shorty. Fuck that nigga!" Piru said, nodding at the man in the middle of the street.

"Santana, my name is Detective Lawson. I know what is going on. Please let me help you."

Detective Lawson tried yet again. Santana looked up at him but walked toward the Caprice. Piru waited to see what the detective was going to do. Detective Lawson continued to walk across the street. Piru looked at Santana. Piru opened the passenger side door and leaned over the roof of the car and opened fire on Lawson. Lawson back-pedaled and pulled his own weapon. He fired back without looking. Santana pulled his Glock and opened fire too. Lawson fell from the bullets that connected with his back. Both Piru and Santana stopped shooting.

"Nigga, hurry the fuck up!" Santana heard Hood Ru yell. Without a second thought Santana rushed to the car. He hopped in and the trio drove away, leaving the detective fighting for his life.

***

Simfany sat in the kitchen with her head in her hands as she thought about what she did. It wasn't about Jimdog no more; that nigga was gone. It was about Santana and the charges he was facing. It was always her that got him into some shit. She would use her money to get him out of the state; that was for sure. She just didn't have anywhere to send him. All her family lived in New York. Simfany was a mess. Her son was again fighting for his life off of the mistakes she made. At the end of the day, it was a good decision for her and her family; the odds just happened to be stacked against the pair. Simfany's phone rang. She picked it up quickly.

"Hello?" she answered.

"Ma, I'm okay. How you been doing?"

"Boy, where are you at? I'm worried about you?"

"I said I'm fine. Anyway, they trying to book me for murdering that hoe ass nigga Jimdog and some nigga named Joseph Wells. I wasn't in the city today, ma, I swear. I don't know why they—" Santana tried to plead his case.

"I know, baby. I believe you. We will get through this. I'm gone call pretty Ricky as soon as I hang up with you. I love you, Santana."

"You don't have to call that nigga. Just come and get me so we can figure out what the fuck we are going to do. Is Paris still there?"

"Nah, it was getting late, so she took Shakira home to bed. You worried about all the wrong shit. Where are you anyway?"

"You know where I'm at ma; just think, I'll be waiting for you. When I see ya Tahoe, I'll come out and get you. It's only three of us in the house so you may have to creep through so we can see you. Oh, and I love you too. See you in a second. Leave now."

"I'm on my way." Simfany hung the phone up and grabbed her keys. She ran to her Tahoe. She knew exactly where Santana was. He was in the Commons. That was the only other place he ever hung out at. Simfany drove cautiously to Harford Commons, hoping not to attract any attention. As she pulled into the complex, she pulled her Tahoe to a slow creep and waited for somebody to come out and direct her to the right spot. She drove another couple seconds before she saw someone appear from behind a small townhouse. Simfany pulled over and parked her car. She rolled her window down as the person walked up. She recognized him.

"Piru, where Santana at?" she asked

"Lor yo inside waiting on you," Piru answered.

"Okay, give me a second. I'm coming." Piru walked away, into the house he snuck from behind. Simfany knew she wouldn't need it, but she grabbed her Glock out of habit. She checked the clip before she exited the car to make sure everything was everything. Simfany walked across the street to the town house and knocked on the door. Piru opened the door laughing.

"Nigga, what the fuck you laughing at?" Simfany joked.

"Why did you knock on the door?"

"Because—Shut up, Piru. I don't know."

"Nigga, leave my mom alone. Come in, ma. I'll be ready in just a second." Simfany sat on the couch that was positioned across from the TV. She crossed her legs and waited.

Santana came from the back with another person that looked familiar as hell. Simfany just couldn't place him. She played her position and waited on Santana to introduce him. It was like Santana read her mind because as soon as the other nigga got comfortable, he spoke.

"My nigga, this mom Dukes—and ma, this my nigga *Stacks*. You already know Piru's crazy ass." Simfany's heart jumped a beat. She couldn't see the dude's face like that, but that wasn't shit; all she need was to hear his voice.

"So, where you from, Stacks?" Simfany asked.

"I'm from the city but I been down here since I was a lor nigga."

"That's what's up. You make sure you take care of my son while he in ya presence. Please. You owe me that much." Simfany rose from her seat. She may have been wrong but her body wasn't. She was scared of Stacks, and she knew why. She found who shot her. She knew the voice all too well. She might have not remembered much, but his voice she did. Simfany began to sweat heavily. She was nervous and scared for both her and Santana.

"Ma, you a'ight?" Santana asked.

"Yeah, baby, my heart just racing from all the adrenaline of the day," Simfany answered. That put Santana on point. He understood what she was saying. Piru walked from the back with a couple of jars of that good ready to blow the walls down. He walked into the room and felt tension. He looked at Santana, Simfany then Stacks. Nobody said anything. Simfany took it for what it was worth and spoke her mind.

"So, Stacks, you knew my nigga, right?"

"Who?"

"Byrd?"

"Kind of in a business type of way. He was an a'ight nigga. I heard his bitch had him smoked."

Simfany laughed. She slowly reached for her waist and pulled her Glock out, raising it to the level of Stacks' face. Without hesitation Piru pulled his gun and trained it on Simfany. Santana looked at Piru and it hurt his heart the minute he pulled his own gun and trained it on his best friend. Three guns aimed and ready to kill each intended target. The look on Simfany's face changed. She looked at Piru, then back at a seated Stacks. She continued.

"So, what made you come to my doorstep and shoot me?" she asked. She needed to know the answer.

"I don't know what you're talking about, shorty. Santana, tell ya mom to put her tone away. She tripping. I ain't have shit—"

"Nah, my nigga, let her finish. I want to know what the fuck is going on too!" Piru stated. Stacks hit him with a look.

"Nigga, don't look at me like that. I got you, my nigga. Never doubt my loyalty. She shoot, I shoot, Santana shoot. Fuck it all for the love of the hood, right!" Piru explained.

"Why did you shoot me, Stacks? You're going to die today, even if I gotta go with you. So, you might as well speak ya peace." Stacks laughed.

"See, that's the tough ass shit that got that nigga Byrd killed. You want to know why I came and tried to smoke you personally. Okay, first off, I know you got killer in ya bloodline. Plus, you were fucking with one of the most feared niggas in Murdaland. He played his part until he thought he was too untouchable. Words were exchanged, so I took it where it needed to be. It just so happened to be an issue between him and Carlos. That gave me enough time to do me and stay under the radar. Now you, on the other hand, I was afraid of. Not in the literal sense of course, but I thought Byrd might have told you something to connect me to him. I got a ruthless team but we can't add up to what Carlos can get. I wasn't ready for a war with Carlos. That shit cost money and soldiers I didn't have, so I tried to kill the only thing connecting me to him. That's enough for you, Simfany." Stacks smiled. He knew it was nothing he could do. He just put his faith in Piru to pull his trigger after she pulled hers. A lone tear rolled down her face for Byrd. She understood the life he lived, and she respected the karma that came with it. The only thing that bothered her was how all the niggas that loved each other killed one another. It was confusing but real.

"Well, since you're being truthful, did you have anything to do with Jimdog trying to fire on my son?"

"To be honest I got nothing but love for Santana. That lor nigga got a lot of heart. I was warned about him and the possibility of this situation coming to fruition, but I play my cards how their dealt. Karma's a motherfucker. But I had nothing to do with that shit between Santana and Jimdog. What are the odds of you finding me?" He laughed at his fate.

"Believe it or not, you found me when you had ya people drop them blue bandannas on Blaze and his mother. Remember that's what you did to me. I'm guessing I was the first. Bitch ass niggas.

That's shit crazy." Simfany's attitude turned cool. Piru looked at Santana, Santana looked at Stacks. Stacks smiled; he couldn't survive this fate. It was written in stone.

"It is what it is, shorty, kill or be killed," Stacks said, knowing they would be his last words in life. "Say no more!" *Boc—Boc—Boc—Boc—Boc—Boc—Boc—Boc—*

To Be Continued...
For the Love of Blood 3
Coming Soon

Lock Down Publications and Ca$h Presents assisted
publishing packages.

BASIC PACKAGE $499
Editing
Cover Design
Formatting

UPGRADED PACKAGE $800
Typing
Editing
Cover Design
Formatting

ADVANCE PACKAGE $1,200
Typing
Editing
Cover Design
Formatting
Copyright registration
Proofreading
Upload book to Amazon

LDP SUPREME PACKAGE $1,500
Typing
Editing
Cover Design
Formatting
Copyright registration
Proofreading
Set up Amazon account
Upload book to Amazon
Advertise on LDP Amazon and Facebook page

***Other services available upon request. Additional
charges may apply
**Lock Down Publications
P.O. Box 944
Stockbridge, GA 30281-9998
Phone # 470 303-9761**

Submission Guideline

Submit the first three chapters of your completed manuscript to ldpsubmissions@gmail.com, subject line: Your book's title. The manuscript must be in a .doc file and sent as an attachment. Document should be in Times New Roman, double spaced and in size 12 font. Also, provide your synopsis and full contact information. If sending multiple submissions, they must each be in a separate email.

Have a story but no way to send it electronically? You can still submit to LDP/Ca$h Presents. Send in the first three chapters, written or typed, of your completed manuscript to:

LDP: Submissions Dept
Po Box 944
Stockbridge, Ga 30281

DO NOT send original manuscript. Must be a duplicate.

Provide your synopsis and a cover letter containing your full contact information.

Thanks for considering LDP and Ca$h Presents.

<u>NEW RELEASES</u>

HOOD CONSIGLIERE 2 by KEESE

KILLA KOUNTY by KHUFU

BETRAYAL OF A THUG 2 by FRE$H

THE COCAINE PRINCESS 5 by KING RIO

FOR THE LOVE OF BLOOD 2 by JAMEL MITCHELL

For the Love of Blood 2

Jamel Mitchell

STRAIGHT BEAST MODE III

De'Kari

KINGPIN KILLAZ IV

STREET KINGS III

PAID IN BLOOD III

CARTEL KILLAZ IV

DOPE GODS III

Hood Rich

SINS OF A HUSTLA II

ASAD

RICH $AVAGE III

By Martell Troublesome Bolden

YAYO V

Bred In The Game 2

S. Allen

THE STREETS WILL TALK II

By Yolanda Moore

SON OF A DOPE FIEND III

HEAVEN GOT A GHETTO II

SKI MASK MONEY II

By Renta

LOYALTY AIN'T PROMISED III

By Keith Williams

I'M NOTHING WITHOUT HIS LOVE II

SINS OF A THUG II

TO THE THUG I LOVED BEFORE II

IN A HUSTLER I TRUST II

By Monet Dragun

QUIET MONEY IV

EXTENDED CLIP III

THUG LIFE IV

By **Trai'Quan**

THE STREETS MADE ME IV

By **Larry D. Wright**

IF YOU CROSS ME ONCE II

ANGEL V

By **Anthony Fields**

THE STREETS WILL NEVER CLOSE IV

By K'ajji

HARD AND RUTHLESS III

KILLA KOUNTY IV

By Khufu

MONEY GAME III

By Smoove Dolla

JACK BOYS VS DOPE BOYS IV

A GANGSTA'S QUR'AN V

COKE GIRLZ II

COKE BOYS II

LIFE OF A SAVAGE V

CHI'RAQ GANGSTAS V

By Romell Tukes

MURDA WAS THE CASE III

Elijah R. Freeman

THE STREETS NEVER LET GO III

By Robert Baptiste

AN UNFORESEEN LOVE IV

BABY, I'M WINTERTIME COLD II

By **Meesha**

MONEY MAFIA II

Jamel Mitchell

For the Love of Blood 2

By Corey Robinson

IT'S JUST ME AND YOU II

By Ah'Million

BORN IN THE GRAVE II

By Self Made Tay

FOREVER GANGSTA III

By Adrian Dulan

GORILLAZ IN THE TRENCHES II

By SayNoMore

THE COCAINE PRINCESS VI

By King Rio

<u>**Available Now**</u>

RESTRAINING ORDER **I & II**

By **CA$H & Coffee**

LOVE KNOWS NO BOUNDARIES **I II & III**

By **Coffee**

RAISED AS A GOON I, II, III & IV

BRED BY THE SLUMS I, II, III

BLAST FOR ME I & II

ROTTEN TO THE CORE I II III

A BRONX TALE I, II, III

DUFFLE BAG CARTEL I II III IV V VI

Jamel Mitchell

HEARTLESS GOON I II III IV V

A SAVAGE DOPEBOY I II

DRUG LORDS I II III

CUTTHROAT MAFIA I II

KING OF THE TRENCHES

By **Ghost**

LAY IT DOWN **I & II**

LAST OF A DYING BREED I II

BLOOD STAINS OF A SHOTTA I & II III

By **Jamaica**

LOYAL TO THE GAME I II III

LIFE OF SIN I, II III

By **TJ & Jelissa**

BLOODY COMMAS I & II

SKI MASK CARTEL I II & III

KING OF NEW YORK I II,III IV V

RISE TO POWER I II III

COKE KINGS I II III IV V

BORN HEARTLESS I II III IV

KING OF THE TRAP I II

By **T.J. Edwards**

IF LOVING HIM IS WRONG…I & II

LOVE ME EVEN WHEN IT HURTS I II III

By **Jelissa**

WHEN THE STREETS CLAP BACK I & II III

THE HEART OF A SAVAGE I II III IV

MONEY MAFIA

LOYAL TO THE SOIL I II III

By **Jibril Williams**

A DISTINGUISHED THUG STOLE MY HEART I II & III

For the Love of Blood 2

LOVE SHOULDN'T HURT I II III IV

RENEGADE BOYS I II III IV

PAID IN KARMA I II III

SAVAGE STORMS I II III

AN UNFORESEEN LOVE I II III

BABY, I'M WINTERTIME COLD

By **Meesha**

A GANGSTER'S CODE I &, II III

A GANGSTER'S SYN I II III

THE SAVAGE LIFE I II III

CHAINED TO THE STREETS I II III

BLOOD ON THE MONEY I II III

A GANGSTA'S PAIN I II

By J-Blunt

PUSH IT TO THE LIMIT

By **Bre' Hayes**

BLOOD OF A BOSS **I, II, III, IV, V**

SHADOWS OF THE GAME

TRAP BASTARD

By **Askari**

THE STREETS BLEED MURDER **I, II & III**

THE HEART OF A GANGSTA I II& III

By **Jerry Jackson**

CUM FOR ME I II III IV V VI VII VIII

An **LDP Erotica Collaboration**

BRIDE OF A HUSTLA **I II & II**

THE FETTI GIRLS **I, II& III**

CORRUPTED BY A GANGSTA I, II III, IV

BLINDED BY HIS LOVE

THE PRICE YOU PAY FOR LOVE I, II ,III

Jamel Mitchell

DOPE GIRL MAGIC I II III
By **Destiny Skai**
WHEN A GOOD GIRL GOES BAD
By **Adrienne**
THE COST OF LOYALTY I II III
By Kweli
A GANGSTER'S REVENGE **I II III & IV**
THE BOSS MAN'S DAUGHTERS I II III IV V
A SAVAGE LOVE **I & II**
BAE BELONGS TO ME I II
A HUSTLER'S DECEIT I, II, III
WHAT BAD BITCHES DO I, II, III
SOUL OF A MONSTER I II III
KILL ZONE
A DOPE BOY'S QUEEN I II III
TIL DEATH
By **Aryanna**
A KINGPIN'S AMBITON
A KINGPIN'S AMBITION **II**
I MURDER FOR THE DOUGH
By **Ambitious**
TRUE SAVAGE I II III IV V VI VII
DOPE BOY MAGIC I, II, III
MIDNIGHT CARTEL I II III
CITY OF KINGZ I II
NIGHTMARE ON SILENT AVE
THE PLUG OF LIL MEXICO II
CLASSIC CITY
By **Chris Green**
A DOPEBOY'S PRAYER

For the Love of Blood 2

By **Eddie "Wolf" Lee**

THE KING CARTEL **I, II & III**

By **Frank Gresham**

THESE NIGGAS AIN'T LOYAL **I, II & III**

By **Nikki Tee**

GANGSTA SHYT **I II &III**

By **CATO**

THE ULTIMATE BETRAYAL

By **Phoenix**

BOSS'N UP **I , II & III**

By **Royal Nicole**

I LOVE YOU TO DEATH

By **Destiny J**

I RIDE FOR MY HITTA

I STILL RIDE FOR MY HITTA

By **Misty Holt**

LOVE & CHASIN' PAPER

By **Qay Crockett**

TO DIE IN VAIN

SINS OF A HUSTLA

By **ASAD**

BROOKLYN HUSTLAZ

By **Boogsy Morina**

BROOKLYN ON LOCK I & II

By **Sonovia**

GANGSTA CITY

By **Teddy Duke**

A DRUG KING AND HIS DIAMOND I & II III

A DOPEMAN'S RICHES

HER MAN, MINE'S TOO I, II

Jamel Mitchell

CASH MONEY HO'S

THE WIFEY I USED TO BE I II

PRETTY GIRLS DO NASTY THINGS

By Nicole Goosby

TRAPHOUSE KING **I II & III**

KINGPIN KILLAZ I II III

STREET KINGS I II

PAID IN BLOOD **I II**

CARTEL KILLAZ I II III

DOPE GODS I II

By **Hood Rich**

LIPSTICK KILLAH **I, II, III**

CRIME OF PASSION I II & III

FRIEND OR FOE I II III

By **Mimi**

STEADY MOBBN' **I, II, III**

THE STREETS STAINED MY SOUL I II III

By **Marcellus Allen**

WHO SHOT YA **I, II, III**

SON OF A DOPE FIEND I II

HEAVEN GOT A GHETTO

SKI MASK MONEY

Renta

GORILLAZ IN THE BAY **I II III IV**

TEARS OF A GANGSTA I II

3X KRAZY I II

STRAIGHT BEAST MODE I II

DE'KARI

TRIGGADALE I II III

MURDAROBER WAS THE CASE I II

188

For the Love of Blood 2

Elijah R. Freeman
GOD BLESS THE TRAPPERS I, II, III
THESE SCANDALOUS STREETS I, II, III
FEAR MY GANGSTA I, II, III IV, V
THESE STREETS DON'T LOVE NOBODY I, II
BURY ME A G I, II, III, IV, V
A GANGSTA'S EMPIRE I, II, III, IV
THE DOPEMAN'S BODYGAURD I II
THE REALEST KILLAZ I II III
THE LAST OF THE OGS I II III
Tranay Adams
THE STREETS ARE CALLING
Duquie Wilson
MARRIED TO A BOSS I II III
By Destiny Skai & Chris Green
KINGZ OF THE GAME I II III IV V VI
Playa Ray
SLAUGHTER GANG I II III
RUTHLESS HEART I II III
By Willie Slaughter
FUK SHYT
By Blakk Diamond
DON'T F#CK WITH MY HEART I II
By Linnea
ADDICTED TO THE DRAMA I II III
IN THE ARM OF HIS BOSS II
By Jamila
YAYO I II III IV
A SHOOTER'S AMBITION I II
BRED IN THE GAME

Jamel Mitchell

By S. Allen

TRAP GOD I II III

RICH $AVAGE I II

MONEY IN THE GRAVE I II III

By Martell Troublesome Bolden

FOREVER GANGSTA I II

GLOCKS ON SATIN SHEETS I II

By Adrian Dulan

TOE TAGZ I II III IV

LEVELS TO THIS SHYT I II

IT'S JUST ME AND YOU

By Ah'Million

KINGPIN DREAMS I II III

RAN OFF ON DA PLUG

By Paper Boi Rari

CONFESSIONS OF A GANGSTA I II III IV

CONFESSIONS OF A JACKBOY I II

By Nicholas Lock

I'M NOTHING WITHOUT HIS LOVE

SINS OF A THUG

TO THE THUG I LOVED BEFORE

A GANGSTA SAVED XMAS

IN A HUSTLER I TRUST

By Monet Dragun

CAUGHT UP IN THE LIFE I II III

THE STREETS NEVER LET GO I II

By Robert Baptiste

NEW TO THE GAME I II III

MONEY, MURDER & MEMORIES I II III

By **Malik D. Rice**

For the Love of Blood 2

LIFE OF A SAVAGE I II III IV
A GANGSTA'S QUR'AN I II III IV
MURDA SEASON I II III
GANGLAND CARTEL I II III
CHI'RAQ GANGSTAS I II III IV
KILLERS ON ELM STREET I II III
JACK BOYZ N DA BRONX I II III
A DOPEBOY'S DREAM I II III
JACK BOYS VS DOPE BOYS I II III
COKE GIRLZ
COKE BOYS
By Romell Tukes
LOYALTY AIN'T PROMISED I II
By Keith Williams
QUIET MONEY I II III
THUG LIFE I II III
EXTENDED CLIP I II
A GANGSTA'S PARADISE
By **Trai'Quan**
THE STREETS MADE ME I II III
By **Larry D. Wright**
THE ULTIMATE SACRIFICE I, II, III, IV, V, VI
KHADIFI
IF YOU CROSS ME ONCE
ANGEL I II III IV
IN THE BLINK OF AN EYE
By **Anthony Fields**
THE LIFE OF A HOOD STAR
By Ca$h & Rashia Wilson
THE STREETS WILL NEVER CLOSE I II III

Jamel Mitchell

By K'ajji

CREAM I II III

THE STREETS WILL TALK

By Yolanda Moore

NIGHTMARES OF A HUSTLA I II III

By King Dream

CONCRETE KILLA I II III

VICIOUS LOYALTY I II

By Kingpen

HARD AND RUTHLESS I II

MOB TOWN 251

THE BILLIONAIRE BENTLEYS I II III

By Von Diesel

GHOST MOB

Stilloan Robinson

MOB TIES I II III IV V VI

SOUL OF A HUSTLER, HEART OF A KILLER

GORILLAZ IN THE TRENCHES

By SayNoMore

BODYMORE MURDERLAND I II III

THE BIRTH OF A GANGSTER I II

By Delmont Player

FOR THE LOVE OF A BOSS

By C. D. Blue

MOBBED UP I II III IV

THE BRICK MAN I II III IV

THE COCAINE PRINCESS I II III IV V

By King Rio

KILLA KOUNTY I II III IV

By Khufu

For the Love of Blood 2

MONEY GAME I II

By Smoove Dolla

A GANGSTA'S KARMA I II

By FLAME

KING OF THE TRENCHES I II III

by **GHOST & TRANAY ADAMS**

QUEEN OF THE ZOO I II

By **Black Migo**

GRIMEY WAYS I II

By Ray Vinci

XMAS WITH AN ATL SHOOTER

By Ca$h & Destiny Skai

KING KILLA

By Vincent "Vitto" Holloway

BETRAYAL OF A THUG I II

By Fre$h

THE MURDER QUEENS I II

By Michael Gallon

TREAL LOVE

By Le'Monica Jackson

FOR THE LOVE OF BLOOD I II

By Jamel Mitchell

HOOD CONSIGLIERE I II

By Keese

PROTÉGÉ OF A LEGEND

By Corey Robinson

BORN IN THE GRAVE

By Self Made Tay

MOAN IN MY MOUTH

By XTASY

Jamel Mitchell

TORN BETWEEN A GANGSTER AND A GENTLEMAN
By J-BLUNT & Miss Kim

BOOKS BY LDP'S CEO, CA$H

TRUST IN NO MAN

TRUST IN NO MAN 2

TRUST IN NO MAN 3

BONDED BY BLOOD

SHORTY GOT A THUG

THUGS CRY

THUGS CRY 2

THUGS CRY 3

TRUST NO BITCH

TRUST NO BITCH 2

TRUST NO BITCH 3

TIL MY CASKET DROPS

RESTRAINING ORDER

RESTRAINING ORDER 2

IN LOVE WITH A CONVICT

LIFE OF A HOOD STAR

XMAS WITH AN ATL SHOOTER

Jamel Mitchell

www.ingramcontent.com/pod-product-compliance
Lightning Source LLC
Chambersburg PA
CBHW070511260626
47161CB00004B/1516